HEIDI BETTS

ON THE VERGE OF VERGE OF I DO

Harlequin®

Desire

Special thanks and acknowledgment to Heidi Betts
for her contribution to the
Dynasties: The Kincaids miniseries.

ISBN-13: 978-0-373-73163-3

ON THE VERGE OF I DO

Recycling programs
for this product may
not exist in your area.

With thanks to JoAnn Ross and Geremy Kephart for all the great Charleston and Hilton Head information you provided. I may not have used it all, but you helped me with this story more than you can know, and I really, *really* appreciate it!

* * *

Don't miss a single book in this series!

Dynasties: The Kincaids
New money. New passions. Old secrets.

HEIDI BETTS

An avid romance reader since junior high, national bestselling author Heidi Betts knew early on that she wanted to write these wonderful stories of love and adventure. It wasn't until her freshman year of college, however, when she spent the entire night before finals reading a romance novel instead of studying, that she decided to take the road less traveled and follow her dream.

Soon after Heidi joined Romance Writers of America, her writing began to garner attention, including placing in the esteemed Golden Heart competition three years in a row. The recipient of numerous awards and stellar reviews, Heidi's books combine believable characters with compelling plotlines, and are consistently described as "delightful," "sizzling" and "wonderfully witty."

For news, fun and information about upcoming books, be sure to visit Heidi online at HeidiBetts.com.

One

"This is a lot of work. I don't know how you do it on a daily basis."

Kara Kincaid chuckled as she turned another page of the catering catalog spread open on the glossy surface of the low black lacquer coffee table in front of them.

"And I don't know how you keep half a dozen luxury hotels and resorts up and running. I'd rather pore over guest lists and seven-course menus any day than try to keep all of that afloat," she told her older sister's fiancé.

Eli Houghton was tall and handsome and mouth-wateringly well-built. With chocolate-brown eyes and wind-blown, coffee-brown hair, the man could make a woman's heart skip a beat without even trying. When he did try...well, that was enough to stop a woman's heart from beating entirely.

"You're selling yourself short, darlin'," he told her, flashing a smile that made her own internal organs do things she didn't think her personal physician would approve of. "We may have different talents, but we've both managed to build successful businesses for ourselves."

"Except that Houghton Hotels and Resorts is worth millions of dollars, and I run Prestige Events out of my home office."

They were sitting on a black leather sofa in Eli's impressive ninth-floor office, but ordinarily they would be having this meeting in the small ground-floor library-turned-workplace of her meticulously restored circa 1806 French Quarter row house on Queen Street.

She loved the quaint, three-bedroom/three-bath home, which was more than enough space for a single gal like herself. But she did sometimes worry that running her business out of her home gave the wrong impression to potential clients. Not for the first time, she realized that she should probably give some serious consideration to renting an office elsewhere.

Possibly even an entire building where she could host tastings, put up displays and store reusable decorations so she wouldn't have to rent them from vendors. She might hire an assistant—or even *employees,* plural, one day—to help her, since she'd been running things pretty much single-handedly so far.

She didn't regret the hard work. Prestige Events was, after all, her baby. The business she'd started on her own, stepping away from her family's interests in shipping and real estate to do it. But it might be nice, just once, to not have to be responsible for *everything,* for everyone else. Or at the very least, to have a handful of workers on staff that she could turn to when two arms, two legs, two ears and one mouth just didn't seem to be enough to get the job done on time.

"Give it time, sugar," Eli said in a voice as smooth as Kentucky bourbon, drawing her attention back to their conversation. "Keep doing what you're doing, and I'd be willing to bet that in a few years you'll be planning the wedding of one of the Obama girls."

Oh, her sister was a lucky, lucky woman. It was a good thing Kara was sitting down. The man oozed charm, and his softly spoken encouragement had her bones melting like butter on a biscuit.

Clearing her throat, she took a deep breath and straightened her spine. This was not the time to be going all weak-kneed over a man. Not the time *or* the man.

Eli was Laurel's fiancé, for Pete's sake. In less than a month, the two would be married.

Yes, Kara found Eli attractive. She'd be willing to bet she was no different than any other red-blooded woman in South Carolina—or heck, the entire Eastern seaboard—in that regard.

Yes, she'd sort of had a crush on him from the time they were teenagers. Again, that was no great surprise. Every girl in school had had her eye on the football player.

Well, almost every girl, anyway. Kara couldn't remember Laurel ever showing more than a passing interest in him while they were growing up. They'd always been friends—all of them, the entire Kincaid brood and the lone boy who lived with the Youngs on the neighboring estate—but it wasn't until much more recently that the two of them had decided to get engaged.

And Kara was happy for them, truly she was. It just wasn't easy to plan a wedding for her sister and the man for whom she'd spent the past ten years carrying a moderately flickering torch.

But she was doing her best. And her best required putting aside any inner turmoil she might be feeling to pull off what could arguably be considered the Wedding of the Year within Charleston's high society circles. The fact that it was her sister's wedding only raised the stakes, made the event that much more important to Kara, both personally and professionally.

Reaching past the catering brochure, she scooped up her glasses and slid them onto her nose. She didn't really need them, but she always felt more sure-footed with them on, and she could certainly use a little added confidence—not to mention an added barrier between herself and Eli—right now.

"Once you and Laurel decide which proteins you want

for the reception, it will be a lot easier to narrow down your choices. And that will actually be the fun part, since you'll be taste-testing samples before we plan the final menu."

Eli leaned back against the sofa, spreading his arms across the buttery-soft leather and crossing his legs to rest an ankle on the opposite knee. "We should probably leave that up to Laurel. I'd hate for us to have our first fight at the wedding reception just because I told you to order fried chicken instead of crab tarts."

Kara checked her watch. Her sister was already twenty minutes late. They'd purposely agreed to meet at Eli's office so his workday wouldn't be turned upside down, but Laurel's tardiness made it look as though that's exactly what was going to happen.

"She should be here any minute," Kara told him.

With a solemn nod, he said, "I'm sure she will be."

He sounded so certain…and so patient. More patient than Kara suspected she would be, if she were in his shoes.

The truth was, in all her time as an event coordinator, all the times she'd dealt with giddy, nervous, and even monstrously spoiled and demanding brides, she'd never put together a wedding for a woman as distracted and seemingly disinterested as her own sister.

Granted, there was a lot going on with their family at the moment. Bad enough that their father had been brutally murdered late one night in his office by someone who had tried to make it look like a suicide…. Bad enough that they'd discovered only after his death that he'd been leading a double life—and had another adult son with another woman…. But now their own mother, Reginald's rightful widow, had been accused of killing her own husband.

Kara didn't care what secrets her father had been keeping or how hurt her mother might have been when she'd discovered his betrayal. Elizabeth Winthrop Kincaid would never have raised a hand against him. Her mama could barely squish a spider, let alone shoot her husband of nearly forty years in the head.

No, it was an absolute impossibility. And every single one of the Kincaid siblings felt the same; they were one-hundred-percent behind their mother. But tell that to the prosecutors who had accused Elizabeth of murder. Luckily, new information had surfaced about a mysterious man seen entering Reginald's office building the night of the murder, which was enough to get Elizabeth out on bail—for now.

So it was no wonder, really, that Laurel—the oldest Kincaid daughter—had more on her mind than just her upcoming nuptials.

Still, it struck Kara as slightly odd that her sister didn't already have a clear vision of her perfect wedding day. Most women did. Most *girls* did, starting around the age of eight.

Kara had never met a bride who didn't already have wedding colors firmly in mind. Who didn't already have an idea of the type of wedding dress she wanted to wear. (Laurel would be wearing a very traditional 1920s vintage gown in vanilla rather than white lace, but only because Kara had pushed and prodded and dragged her to fittings, essentially demanding her sister make a decision before time ran out.) Who showed up late for each and every scheduled meeting, be it about picking flowers or setting dates for the bachelorette party, rehearsal dinner, and ceremony itself.

She wondered if Eli had noticed his fiancée's peculiar—at least in Kara's opinion—behavior, and if he found it as perplexing as she was beginning to.

From the looks of him, he either hadn't, or Laurel's frequent delays didn't bother him. He seemed totally at ease, even dressed for business, as he was now, in a charcoal suit and pomegranate-red tie.

He also didn't seem the least concerned with how much this wedding was going to cost. Traditionally, the bride's family footed the bill, and the Kincaids could certainly afford to host the celebration. But given the family's current troubling state of affairs and ongoing legal predicament, Eli had told the Kincaids not to worry about it and ordered Kara in no uncertain terms to be sure that all the bills associated with the upcoming nuptials were sent directly to him.

It was a gesture that hadn't surprised Kara. Eli had always been kind and generous and understanding. Growing up in the foster care system, he knew what it was like to have nothing, to go without. But even now that he'd made such a success of himself, he didn't pinch pennies or hoard his millions like a miser.

She only hoped he was still feeling as benevolent once he caught a glimpse of the invoices that were headed his way. The tally was already hovering around the six-figure mark in deposits alone.

As the seconds ticked past, marked by the heavy *tock tock tock* of the antique grandfather clock standing sentinel against the far wall, Kara began to wonder what else she could discuss with Eli that would be wedding-related and not a repeat of previous exchanges. She could probably go back to the beginning of the catering brochure and explain the myriad choices again, in greater detail, but she knew Eli would see that for exactly what it was—a stall tactic.

And then she didn't need to stall, because the office door swung open and Laurel walked in. The epitome of feminine business chic, she was wearing a sage-green skirt and a matching tailored suit jacket the same color as her eyes over a white blouse. On her feet were stylish but practical taupe pumps, and her long, dark auburn hair hung around her shoulders and down her back with just a touch of curl at the ends.

Like their mother, Laurel was a true beauty. She could stop traffic with just a look, and had always had her choice of handsome and attentive beaux. Though until Eli, she'd never seemed willing to settle on any of them.

"Sorry I'm late," she murmured, not making eye contact with either Kara or her fiancé as she slipped a pair of oversize sunglasses into her designer handbag.

Eli, who had gotten up the minute she'd entered, went to her and gave her a quick peck on the cheek. "Don't worry, your sister has been keeping me plenty entertained. Apparently, we have more than three hundred different choices when it comes to entrées, each of which Kara was more than happy to describe in detail."

He turned back to Kara with a smile. "Details I'm sure she'll be regaling you with next."

He didn't seem the least bit put out at the prospect of hearing her catering spiel all over again, which prompted her to return his smile.

The corners of Laurel's mouth lifted in response, but her eyes were flat, her expression tense. Her fingers clutched the strap of her purse so tightly her knuckles were white.

"Can we talk?" she asked Eli in a low voice. Then to Kara, she said, "I'm sorry, but can we do this another time? I really need to speak with Eli."

"Of course," Kara replied, getting quickly to her feet to gather her things.

Folders under her arm and portfolio in hand, she started for the door, but paused before the couple. Eli still looked completely at ease, but tension radiated from Laurel in waves, and Kara tried without words, sister to sister, to convey her concern and ask if everything was all right, if there was anything she could do.

"Call me when you're ready to reschedule," she told them simply, offering Eli a short nod and brushing her hand encouragingly down her sister's arm as she continued on her way.

Closing the door behind her with a soft click, she hoped everything was all right and knew she would be calling her sister to find out what was going on as soon as she got home.

From the look on Laurel's face, and the fact that she'd sent her sister away, Eli knew something was wrong. He just hoped it was nothing too awful. Laurel and the rest of the Kincaid family had had a hell of a year already; he honestly wasn't sure she—or they—could take much more.

Then again, if whatever had his fiancée's Southern belle skin turning even paler was connected to her father's murder and her mother's subsequent arrest for the crime, or anything else related to her family's recent troubles, surely she would have shared the news with her sister rather than asking Kara to leave so they could talk privately. That prospect had his brow puckering and the wheels in his head turning at a rapid pace.

"Here, come sit down," he said, taking her hand and drawing her over to the sofa he and Kara had so recently vacated. Her long, slim, perfectly manicured fingers were chilly against his own, her movements stiff as she sat.

"Is everything all right?" he asked, suspecting it wasn't when she refused to meet his eyes.

"I'm sorry, Eli," she said, her voice wavering slightly. Her dark auburn hair fell around her face and shoulders like a shroud, shifting only when she finally raised her gaze to his. Taking a deep breath, she seemed to steel herself for whatever it was she was about to tell him.

"I'm sorry," she said again, the words rushing together, "but I don't think I can do this. I don't think I can go through with the wedding."

For a second, Eli was certain he'd heard her wrong. Maybe his mind had been on something else, and her words had gotten jumbled with his wayward thoughts.

"Excuse me?"

In a burst of energy unlike any she'd shown since arriving at his office, Laurel jumped up, letting her purse fall to the floor while she skirted the coffee table and began to pace. Back and forth, back and forth, long, agitated strides wearing a path in front of his desk.

"This was a mistake," she said, twisting her hands together at her waist, keeping her gaze straight ahead as she spoke. "We rushed into things. And even though it seemed like a good idea at the time, circumstances have changed."

Stopping on a dime, she turned to him, her arms falling to her sides. "My life is a mess right now, Eli. My father has been murdered, my mother was accused of killing him, I've suddenly got one new half brother and another step-*ish* brother I didn't know existed…"

He'd never heard a woman's voice be both strong and weak at the same time, but hers was. Her words were filled with conviction, even as emotion caused them to tremble.

"You've been amazingly supportive, and I know Mama has been keeping a stiff upper lip. She always wears a smile, tells us everything will be fine, insists we go forward with the wedding because she doesn't want to admit how precarious the future is—for her, as well as the rest of us."

She took a breath, her chest rising as she drew air in, then blew it out again on a sigh. "But I don't think I can do that. Everything isn't okay. My whole world has been turned upside down, and I have no idea what tomorrow might bring. There is just no way I can get married right now, no matter how disappointed people might be. I'm sorry."

Eli sat in silence, watching Laurel's green eyes glisten and the tight line of her mouth quiver while she waited for him to respond.

He wondered if she expected him to be upset. To shoot to his feet and go red in the face as he shouted at her about wasting his time and money. Or maybe to not take no for an answer, insisting that she *would* go through with the wedding, regardless of the nightmare she was currently going through with her family.

He probably should be feeling those things, at least to some degree. He was being dumped, after all. Dumped, jilted, for all intents and purposes, left at the altar. Shouldn't his male pride be rearing on its hind legs, bristling with indignation?

Instead, he found himself not feeling much of anything. He was sitting there, staring at his now *ex*-fiancée, thinking that her eyes weren't quite as vibrant a green as her sister's.

They were pretty, of course. Laurel was, without a doubt,

an extremely lovely woman. Every inch of her, from the crown of her salon-perfect head to the toes of her six-hundred-dollar designer shoes, was the picture of classic, genteel beauty.

But the green of her eyes lent itself more to jade, while Kara's were a deep, glittering green that reminded him of emeralds or South Carolina's own lush salt marshes.

The fact that thoughts like those were even circling in his head at a time like this was probably a fairly good sign that Laurel was absolutely right to call off the wedding. She might be using her family's recent upheaval as an excuse not to go through with it, but he was beginning to think that they simply might not be right for each other.

Their courtship had certainly not been any romantic, whirlwind affair. More precisely, Eli had begun to feel that it was probably time for him to settle down, and Laurel had seemed like a wholly logical choice of wife. They'd grown up together, been friends for years, and when he'd proposed to her—in more of a business proposal than proposal-proposal fashion—she'd accepted with a gentle nod and a kiss to the corner of his mouth.

From there, events had carried along in a very systematic, well-planned manner, just like everything else in both of their very systematic, well-planned lives.

They'd never even slept together. Something that Eli was just now realizing should have been another bright, flashing, fiery red flag. Though at the time, through all the months of their extended engagement, it hadn't seemed unusual at all. Not even for Eli, who considered himself a man with a more-than-healthy sex drive.

Pushing to his feet, he crossed the short distance to Laurel, wrapping his hands around her upper arms, just above her elbows. He stared into her worried eyes for a moment, then leaned in to press a comforting kiss to her cheek.

"I understand," he told her gently, pulling back to offer her an encouraging smile. "Don't worry about a thing. I'll even talk to Kara about cancelling the arrangements. You just take care of yourself, and do whatever you need to in order to be there for your family."

Eli felt, as well as saw, the tension leave Laurel's body. The hard line of her mouth, her stiff spine, and the stillness of her chest while she held her breath all relaxed in a whoosh of relief.

"Thank you," she whispered, letting her head fall against his shoulder. "Thank you so much."

"I want you to be happy, Laurel. I would never want our marriage to feel like a duty or make you *un*happy."

Lifting her head, she smiled up at him, her eyes glittering again, but for a different reason.

"You're a good man, Elijah James Houghton. And one day, you're going to be a wonderful husband to a very lucky woman. I'm only sorry I'm not that woman."

Going up on tiptoe, she bussed the hard line of his jaw before collecting her handbag and letting herself out of the office, leaving him once again alone and woefully unattached.

Two

Eli sat on the far bench seat of his regular booth at Tamblyn's, nursing three fingers of Scotch on the rocks and waiting for his longtime friend, Rakin Abdellah, to arrive.

The two men had met during their days at Harvard Business School, rowing together on the university team and bonding over their mutual lack of immediate family—Eli having been a foster child from a very early age, and Rakin having lost his parents in a light plane accident when he was young. And now they were working together, too, with Rakin's overseas import/export company supplying many of the essential items for Eli's hotels and resorts.

Eli had been at the restaurant for nearly half an hour now, and was on his second glass of Scotch. But Rakin wasn't late—Eli was early.

He'd stayed at the office until his usual quitting time, but couldn't say he'd gotten a hell of a lot done after Laurel dropped her bomb.

He wasn't sorry, exactly, and he certainly didn't blame her.

Even if her personal life hadn't been in upheaval, prompting her to call things off, he wouldn't have wanted her to go through with the wedding unless she felt one-hundred-percent sure it was what she wanted to do. Neither of them deserved to spend the next fifty years in a miserable, loveless marriage.

But he did regret that their engagement had come to an end. There was a certain level of embarrassment involved. The humiliation of having to tell people the wedding they'd expected to attend in only a month's time had been cancelled. Of having to face his friends and business acquaintances and wonder if *they* were wondering what had happened…if he had done the dumping or she had, if he was happy to once again be a free agent or was wallowing in misery.

But more than that, he was disappointed to find himself without a serious relationship prospect.

It wasn't that he was desperate. Lord knew he'd had his fair share of girlfriends, some sticking around longer than others. He'd also had his fair share of one-night stands. Glancing around, he decided he could probably pick up any single woman in this restaurant in about ten minutes flat.

The problem was, he didn't want any of the women in this restaurant. He wasn't sure he'd entirely wanted Laurel—not the way a husband should want a wife. But she'd been a good match for him, and he'd been hopeful that in time, passion would grow.

It wasn't even the idea of being without a woman—a serious girlfriend, an intended, a bride-to-be—that bothered him, it was the extra distance that had been put between him and his desire for a family.

Without a doubt, he loved his foster parents. Warren and Virginia Young had taken him in when he was twelve years old. While most families preferred toddlers or babies, the older couple had been happy to take in a preteen boy and raise him to adulthood. They had even suggested, more than once, that he allow them to adopt him legally.

As much as he appreciated the offer and the deep sentiment

behind it, he'd politely turned them down. They were his parents, and he was their son, in nearly every sense of the word. Absolutely.

But something inside of him would always make him a bit of a lone wolf. He didn't want to take someone else's name, because he wanted to make something of his own. He didn't want anyone to ever look at him and think that he wouldn't have amounted to anything if it hadn't been for the charity of the wealthy, deep-rooted Southern family who had taken him in.

He was sure some folks already thought that, and in all honesty, his prospects probably had improved tenfold when he'd moved in with the Youngs. Without them, he would have been left to languish in the foster care system, and for that, he would always be grateful.

But with the exception of a stable home environment and an Ivy League education, everything he had and everything he'd built, he'd earned and done on his own. Though several million of them had been offered, he hadn't accepted so much as a dime from his parents to start Houghton Hotels and Resorts.

Eli took another sip of the super-smooth Scotch, scanning the front of the restaurant for his still-missing dinner companion. It wasn't yet six o'clock, and Rakin was normally quite prompt, so he was sure his friend would be there soon.

Swirling the remaining liquid at the bottom of his glass, he let his mind drift back to his current situation.

He had solid family roots. He'd created, and was running, a very successful Fortune 500 corporation. Now he found himself yearning for a wife and kids and the whole picket fence American dream—or his adaptation of it, at any rate.

He'd thought marrying Laurel would be the first step toward realizing that dream, but now he'd been forced two steps back.

Ah, well, he had time. He was only thirty-five, after all. And according to statistics, there were plenty of women in the world looking for rich, eligible men. He just had to be careful that when he met one, she was as interested in him as she was in his millions.

"You look deep in thought."

The low male voice caught him by surprise, even though he'd been waiting for Rakin to arrive. Eli lifted his head just as his friend slid into the opposite side of the booth and settled against the soft, russet-colored leather.

Raised for most of his life in Diyafa by his paternal grandparents after his parents were killed, Rakin possessed the jet-black hair, brown eyes and darkly tanned skin of his Middle Eastern heritage. But he was also half-American, which meant he'd spent holidays, vacations and much of his college years in the United States with his mother's family, making him comfortable in either country and both cultures.

"Business troubles?" Rakin asked, raising an arm to signal for the waiter.

"Nothing so simple as that," Eli muttered.

Rakin raised one dark brow in question. They'd been friends long enough that words weren't always necessary. Rakin knew that if something was wrong, and if Eli wanted him to know the details, he would share in his own good time.

"Let's order first," Eli told him, "and discuss that shipment of linens for the Seabrook Island location. Then maybe I'll be ready to tell you about my day." After a bite to eat and a few more fingers of Scotch.

When their waiter appeared, they asked for drinks, then pored over the leather-bound menus until they arrived. Eli knew why he was drinking, of course, but was surprised when Rakin ordered the same. He suspected he might not be the only one having a rough day.

Once their orders had been placed, the two men squared off, hands wrapped around their respective glasses. After a few seconds, one corner of Eli's mouth curved in a grin. Rakin's quickly followed suit. They both chuckled.

"You first," Eli said.

"The linens are on their way," Rakin told him. "Everything

is on schedule. I should have them for you late next week. At the moment, they're scheduled to be delivered directly to Ocean Breezes, but there's still time to change that, if you'd prefer they be delivered to your office here in Charleston."

Eli gave an approving nod, but that's not what he'd meant, and they both knew it.

"And…" he prompted. Partly because he was genuinely interested in what was going on in his friend's life, and partly to buy time until he had to reveal the latest turmoil in his own.

Rakin sighed, dropping his attention to the table. "Grandfather is threatening me with disinheritance."

Eli sat back, eyes going wide. "What? Why?"

Lifting his gaze back to Eli's, Rakin said, "He wants me to marry. He's been pressuring me about it for quite some time, but now he's serious. He wants it done sooner rather than later, and doesn't particularly care about my opinion on the matter."

For a second, Eli didn't say anything, just let the words sink in, the irony of the situation wash over him. Then he let out a bark of laughter.

"This is funny to you," Rakin said. It was a question, but it came out more of a statement—a very disgruntled one.

Eli shook his head. "I'm sorry. It isn't funny. But if you knew what happened to me today, you'd be laughing, too."

"All right, I'll bite. What happened today?"

"Laurel called off the wedding." He said it quickly and succinctly, like tearing off a bandage, then downed the last of his second glass of Scotch.

It was Rakin's turn to look shocked. "What? Why?"

Eli's mouth curved in amusement. Weren't those the exact words he'd uttered only moments before when Rakin had told him about his grandfather's command that he marry? Surely his friend could see the humor in that.

"She says things are too erratic right now, her life too chaotic with everything that's going on with her family."

Rakin inclined his head sagely. "I can understand that, I suppose. The Kincaids certainly have had their share of bad luck lately."

Eli nodded in return. "Agreed. Although I think Laurel's reasons for backing out of the marriage have more to do with her feelings for me than anything that's going on with her family. Her feelings…" he muttered into his empty glass, "or lack thereof."

"You don't think she loves you?" his friend asked quietly.

"I think she cares for me," he answered honestly, "the same way I care for her. As friends. I'm just not sure that's enough to build a marriage on."

Rakin cocked another brow. From the expression on his face, Eli could tell he finally recognized the irony of their situations.

"I guess I'll have to let you know, since I have to enter a loveless marriage or risk being disinherited," Rakin told him.

"Something you're *not* willing to risk, right?"

His friend gave him a look—a cross between *What do you think?* and *Would you?*

As CEO of his family's multi-million-dollar import/export company, Rakin had worked too hard and had too much to lose to gamble that his grandfather would change his mind.

"Well, if you're interested," Eli told him, feeling less troubled than he had since walking into the restaurant, "I can introduce you to a very attractive single young lady from a very respectable Southern family. She was engaged, but I have it on good authority that she jilted her fiancé only a month before they were supposed to exchange vows."

"Yes, I imagine you could," Rakin replied dryly just as the waiter returned with their entrées. Once the young man made sure they had everything they needed and left to refill their drinks—this time, both men switched to coffee—he added, "Let me try one more time to change Grandfather's mind. If I can't, I may just take you up on that."

It was nearly 9 p.m. by the time Eli and Rakin finished dinner and parted ways outside the high-priced restaurant.

Despite the fact that Eli had drunk three Scotch on the rocks straight, he'd then downed a very filling meal and just as many cups of coffee during the rest of the evening, so he was far from intoxicated.

He was also far from in the mood to go home and sit alone for the rest of the night. If he did, he knew he'd only end up opening another bottle of Scotch and starting all over again.

He was restless, and quite frankly, didn't want to be alone. Which didn't mean he was lonely, per se, but as nice as his high-rise luxury apartment was, it would still be empty and too quiet for his current state of mind.

Almost before he'd realized it, he was driving toward the French Quarter, headed for Queen Street. It was late, but there was a chance Kara would still be up. And after all, he had promised Laurel he would take care of informing her sister about the cancelled wedding.

Ten minutes later, he was standing on the stoop of her yellow chiffon row house, raising a hand to the brass knocker on the black lacquered door. The building itself was a couple of hundred years old, but showed no signs of wear. It had been kept up well by the prior owners, and Kara had done quite a bit of work herself to see it fully restored.

Even though most of the trim was painted white, the shutters and wrought-iron window dressings were black to match the front door. Fire-engine-red azaleas sat in giant pots on either side of the steps and hung from every windowsill, bringing the house to bright and summery life.

At least during the day. At night, they simply added more contrast to the already shadowed street.

To be safe, Eli glanced up at the front of the house, not letting the knocker fall until he spotted lights on in an upstairs window. Even then, he didn't knock too loudly in case she'd fallen asleep. If she was awake, he wanted to talk to her, but if she wasn't, he didn't want to disturb her.

The seconds ticked by while he waited, debating whether to knock again. Just as he'd decided to turn around and go home to his empty apartment, the outdoor sconces flipped on. Another beat passed, then he heard the scratch and click of locks being turned and unlatched, and the door swung open.

Kara stood less than a foot away, the yellow cast of light from the front stoop and the far-off upstairs hallway at her back causing a halo effect all around her. Her generous curves were encased in a silky, pearl-white robe covered with purple violets, her chestnut hair falling around her shoulders in a veil of loose, natural curls. A few inches below the hem of her robe, her feet were adorably bare, the nails painted a shimmering shade of seashell pink.

Attraction, sharp and immediate, hit him point-blank in the solar plexus. Knocked the air from his lungs. Damn near rocked him back on his heels. When he could draw a breath, he did, hoping his instant and unexpected lust wasn't written all over his face—not to mention other parts of his body.

Maybe he'd had too much to drink, after all. Wasn't that the only logical excuse for such an intense reaction to his ex-fiancée's sister? Especially when that fiancée was only an ex by a handful of hours.

Then again, maybe his response to the sight of Kara ready for bed was purely that of a man who'd gone too long without the pleasures of a woman's body. And Kara's lush body was one to make any man sit up and take notice.

"Eli," Kara greeted him softly, tiny lines crinkling over her nose as she frowned in confusion. "What are you doing here?"

Resting a hand on the jamb and leaning slightly in that direction, he said, "I'm sorry. It's too late to be dropping by, isn't it?"

She studied him for a moment, raking her gaze from the top of what he suspected was his tousled head, over his tired face, down the line of his disheveled shirt, jacket and dress slacks, and back again.

"Please tell me you didn't drive over here after drinking," she chastised, eyes narrowing with disapproval.

He held up the middle three fingers of his free hand. "Three

Scotches. But that was more than three hours ago, and I've had dinner and several cups of coffee since. I'm sober, I swear." This time, he held his hand up as though taking an oath on a Bible in a court of law.

She considered that for a moment before letting out a soft sigh and taking a step back into the foyer. "You'd better get in here before my neighbors get suspicious," she told him, opening the door wider to allow him entry.

Stuffing his hands in his pockets, he moved inside, waiting for her to close and lock the door behind them. When she turned to face him again, he knew without a doubt that she knew. She knew and felt sorry for him.

"I talked to Laurel," she admitted in little more than a whisper, her gaze hovering somewhere around his chin rather than meeting his eyes. "I'm so sorry."

Dammit, he didn't want her pity. He didn't want anyone's pity. And if this was the reaction his own almost-sister-in-law had, he could only imagine how awful it would be to deal with all of his other friends and acquaintances once they found out Laurel had dumped him.

"Christ," he swore in a manner he almost never did, especially in a lady's presence. "I don't need this."

Running a rough hand through his hair, he started to pace the length of her entryway. His steps tapped out a brusque, staccato trail back and forth across the glossy hardwood floor. "I don't need the rumors or the sympathy or the negative attention this is going to draw. I don't care that she called off the wedding," he charged to no one in particular, "but I damn well don't need the fallout it's going to cause."

He was driving his fingers through his hair again, working himself into a good huff, when Kara touched his arm. That one light touch halted him in his tracks and brought his head around until he met her gaze.

"Let's go into the kitchen," she told him in a gentle voice. "I'll make us some tea, or even pour you another glass of

Scotch, as long as you promise to spend the night here instead of trying to drive yourself home."

And just like that, his tension leeched away. He followed her past the stairwell leading to the second floor and down a long, narrow hallway to the kitchen that ran nearly the entire width of the back of the house.

This wasn't his first time wandering around Kara's home, and not because he'd been here so often recently to discuss wedding plans. When she'd first moved in, the entire family and a few friends—Eli included—had come by to help her unpack. Then later, she'd thrown a housewarming party to show off "her baby" and given everyone the grand tour.

It had been a while, though, since he'd been farther inside than the office she used for Prestige Events at the front of the house, and he had to admit he liked what she'd done with the place. Not only was it neat as a pin, but the decor looked like something that should grace the pages of *Better Homes and Gardens* or *Garden & Gun*.

He wondered briefly if she'd decorated it herself, or hired someone. And then that if she'd done it herself, she could make a hell of a fall-back career for herself if she ever gave up event coordination. Or maybe she could consider expanding Prestige Events into Prestige Events and Interior Design. Lord knew he'd paid an arm and two legs to the woman who had styled his apartment, and it was only about one-third the size of Kara's house.

Leading him into the state-of-the-art kitchen, she glanced at him over her shoulder, sending her curls bouncing. "So what's it going to be—tea or Scotch?"

His mouth opened, but she stopped him from getting a word out with an upheld hand. "Before you answer, I should probably warn you that I don't think I even have Scotch. It's never been my drink of choice. I maybe have a bit of vodka or some gin, but aside from that, your hard liquor choices are somewhat limited."

"If you didn't have Scotch," he said slowly, "why did you offer?"

She lifted one slim shoulder in a shrug. "I wanted you to stay, and didn't know if you would otherwise."

Eli smiled, and he was surprised by how easily his lips curved, how much better he felt just being here with her. "Well, then…tea, it is."

With a short nod, she turned to collect a stainless steel teapot, fill it with water, and put it on to boil. Enjoying the gentle sway of her hips and occasional bounce of her breasts as she moved, he made his way to the island in the middle of the room and pulled out one of the oak stools to take a seat.

Next she collected a delicate china tea service—cups and saucers, teapot, creamer, sugar bowl, a plate for lemon wedges—and set it all on the island in front of him.

"You don't have to go to all this bother," he told her.

She shot him a crooked grin. "This is how tea is done in Charleston, no matter the day or the hour. Mama would faint dead away if she found out I was doing it any other way."

"So no convenient, pre-packaged tea bags dipped into mugs of microwaved water, huh?"

"Hush your mouth," she chastised, letting her natural Southern accent go even deeper. Going to a nearby cupboard, she removed a fancy tin full of loose tea leaves, shaking them at him for emphasis.

Ten minutes later, she was perched on the stool next to him, facing him on the same side of the champagne-marble-topped island. She crossed her legs while she poured the tea, causing her robe to slide open and reveal a long expanse of smooth, alabaster skin from knee to thigh. Eli's gaze zeroed in on that strip of sleek flesh, making his groin tighten and his mouth go dry.

"Something tells me you're not much for tea, no matter how it's prepared," she remarked, handing him a steaming cup on a matching saucer before filling her own.

"Guilty," he admitted. "I'm definitely more of a black coffee kind of guy." Even so, he took a sip of the hot, dark brew. "But I've sat through my fair share of afternoon teas with Mom, so I can hold my own when I need to."

Kara smiled, distractedly rearranging the folds of her robe to cover her legs. More's the pity.

Long moments ticked by in companionable silence, the only sound in the room the ticking of the wall clock hanging over the bank of ovens.

"I really am sorry about what Laurel did," she said suddenly, dragging him straight back down to earth with an unpleasant thud.

He was starting to feel like a broken record, having had a similar conversation with Rakin less than an hour before, but he carefully returned his cup to its saucer and told her the truth. "I'm not. Not really."

Her eyes widened slightly, as though his response surprised her…or she didn't quite believe him.

Making sure to hold her gaze so she could see that he was sincere, he said, "I mean it. I don't want Laurel to marry me if she doesn't *want* to be married to me. That's a recipe for disaster, and the fastest way I can think of for us to end up miserable."

Kara lowered her gaze, using one fingertip to trace around the rim of her tea cup. "But the two of you made such a lovely couple," she murmured. "I know things are kind of crazy with our family right now, but that didn't seem to bother you, and if Laurel loved you…if you loved each other…"

She trailed off, her voice growing to little more than a whisper. Then she lifted her chin, her eyes locking with his. "If you love each other, I wouldn't think there was anything that could keep you from getting married."

Three

Kara didn't know why she'd said that. It was none of her business, and the last thing she wanted to consider too closely was Laurel and Eli's romantic relationship.

Bad enough she'd been writhing with guilt for months over her secret attraction to her sister's fiancé. Now she was bouncing like a Ping-Pong ball between feeling genuinely sorry the engagement had come to an end and being almost relieved, because it meant she wouldn't have to spend the rest of her life watching Laurel and Eli living their happily ever after together.

It would be better for her to keep her mouth shut and play the role of the concerned, but not overly invested wedding planner rather than sister to the ex-bride-to-be and friend to the ex-groom-to-be. She should be more focused on the unraveling of all the wheels that had already been set in motion for the coordination of the Big Day itself than in the myriad emotions involved in the dissolution of such an event.

But she wasn't just any wedding planner. She was also a sister. She was also a friend. And it would be selfish of her to pretend otherwise when Eli, and probably her sister, needed her support and understanding.

The very idea, though, had her stomach in knots. How could she commiserate with Eli when Laurel was her sister? Or with her sister when she was secretly glad Laurel had called off the wedding?

Grabbing her cup, she brought it to her lips and swallowed the piping hot tea in one giant gulp, wishing it were laced with a dash or two of that Scotch Eli had mentioned. Since it wasn't, she reached for the teapot and poured herself another serving... for all the good it would do.

"I think that might be the sticking point," Eli said, toying with his tea more than he was drinking it.

She could feel his eyes drilling into her, willing her to return his gaze. Stomach churning, she wiped her damp palms on her robe and forced herself to do just that.

As always when she looked at him straight-on, her heart did a little swan dive behind her rib cage. She imagined herself having to sit across from him every week at the Kincaids' Sunday family dinners while he was married to Laurel, while he started a family with Laurel...and the small prick of guilt that lived inside her grew to a full-blown cottonwood tree.

Because she was *glad* those encounters were no longer a part of her projected future. She was glad that the rare times Eli joined the family for Sunday dinner—he'd had a standing invitation since they were teens, thanks to her mother—it *wouldn't* be as Laurel's husband.

"We were the perfect couple on paper," he continued. "Both successful. Both from good families, Charleston-born-and-bred. Well, you know..." he said, alluding to his foster child status with a self-deprecating grin. "We would have looked wonderful in all the photographs for the paper and *Garden & Gun*. Our children would have been frighteningly beautiful."

Laurel and Eli's children. Oh, yes, Kara had imagined those, as well. And they *would* have been frighteningly beautiful;

anything else was a genetic impossibility, given their parents' striking good looks.

It was enough to make her want to cry.

"But at best, Laurel and I would have had a good partnership. Almost akin to a savvy business partnership."

Kara frowned. "I don't understand," she said, feeling as though she'd missed something.

"Laurel doesn't love me," he told her point-blank. "Not as more than a friend, at any rate."

Now that he said it, Kara could see the truth of the statement. It explained her sister's disinterest in the details of her own wedding. The dress, the flowers, the guest list, the date... Kara had had to press for decisions and lead Laurel by the hand through every step of the process, something she wouldn't have had to do if Laurel's heart had truly been in it.

Which meant her betrothal to Eli had been one-sided, with all of the love and emotion needed to keep a relationship afloat coming from him.

Oh, this night just kept getting better and better.

Licking her lips, she forced herself to whisper the words she was far from feeling. "I'm sorry."

Eli gave a sharp shake of his head. "Don't be. It has nothing to do with you, and I'm better off coming to terms with this now instead of a couple years into the marriage."

A short pause and then, "What did Laurel say when she told you?"

"Just that the wedding was called off," she answered honestly. "By her, because of everything that's going on with Mama, and Daddy's murder investigation, et cetera. She didn't seem inclined to say more, and I didn't press."

She took a sip from her second cup of tea before it grew cold, then offered him a weak smile. "This is new territory for me, and I'm afraid I'm not quite sure how to properly balance the fine line between sister and wedding planner. Or friend and wedding planner, either."

He returned her lopsided grin with one of his own. "Have

you ever had to deal with a situation like this before in your line of work?"

Kara shook her head so hard and so fast she nearly gave herself whiplash. "I've dealt with demanding brides and even more demanding mothers-of-the-bride. Grooms with cold feet. I've had bar mitzvahs canceled or anniversary parties rescheduled at the last minute. But this…this is all very new to me. Until now, all of the weddings I've been involved with have gone off with only the usual number of minor, to-be-expected hitches. Which is maybe why I should have recused myself from planning this one from the beginning."

"Recused yourself?" he repeated, poking fun at her choice of words.

"You know what I mean," she told him. Her tone was light, the same as his, and for the first time all night, she felt her chest loosen, some of the tension in the room ease. "I should have recommended another wedding planner and just stuck with being a bridesmaid."

Eli quirked one coffee-colored brow. "But then I'd be sitting in some other woman's kitchen, and I'll bet she wouldn't know how to pull off a proper Southern tea service."

His tone was low and suggestive, at least to Kara's ears, rolling through her veins like warm honey. Lord have mercy, the man was a danger to female hormones everywhere.

Once she found her tongue and thought she could speak without sounding like she lived deep, *deep* in the bayou, she said, "Well, I'm glad you felt comfortable coming here. Even if we both know you'd prefer Scotch over a cup of hot tea."

She flashed him a tentative grin, and was rewarded by a chuckle of agreement.

"I do have sweet tea," she told him, "if you'd prefer that."

Leaning back an inch or two, he glanced at the bit of china as though it were a tightly coiled snake, then at her. "Am I that transparent?"

"Not at all." She hopped off her stool and rounded the island to retrieve a glass from the cupboard, then ice cubes and a pitcher of chilled sweet tea from the stainless steel refrigerator.

"I've seen lots of things more transparent than you," she added as she set the filled glass and pitcher in front of him. "Windows. Water. Cellophane…"

"Yeah, yeah, I get it. You can read me like a book." He downed half the glass in one long swallow, then released a satisfied sigh before returning it to the countertop with a soft clink. "But I really am glad you're our event coordinator. It will be a lot easier to go through the process of dismantling everything with you than with a near-stranger."

She inclined her head. She'd never had to completely undo all the plans for such a large event, but she would do everything she could to see that it went smoothly, and that it had as little impact on Eli and Laurel as possible.

"So where do we start as far as that's concerned, anyway?" he asked.

She blinked, caught off guard by the question.

"You want to talk about that tonight?" She was surprised he wanted to talk about the end of the engagement at all so soon, let alone the steps that would need to be taken to cancel the wedding.

"Why not?" he replied with a shrug. And then he let his gaze slide down the length of her body and back up again. "Unless you wanted to get to bed. I really shouldn't have dropped in on you so late."

He put one foot on the floor, prepared to stand up and let himself out, but she stopped him with a hand on his wrist.

"Don't go," she told him, feeling her throat close with unexpected emotion. "It's fine. My only plans for tomorrow were to…" She trailed off, not entirely sure how to finish that sentence.

"Work on more of the arrangements for the wedding?" he supplied wryly.

She gave a reluctant nod.

"Well, the good news," he said, sounding cheerier than she

would have expected, "is that you don't have to change your plans. Just alter them a little to start *cancelling* the arrangements instead of setting them up."

"As long as you seem to be in a fairly good mood," she said, "I should warn you that the chances I'll be able to get your deposits back are slim to none. They're non-refundable, and of course I'll do my best to talk the vendors into reconsidering, but—"

"Don't worry about it," he cut her off to say. Then when she didn't respond, he added, "I expected as much. And even though it's no small amount of money, I'd rather let it go than add to your stress level by making you fight to get it back."

"Are you sure?" she asked quietly. It was a very substantial "no small amount" of money; anyone else would be livid at the thought of losing it.

Taking another drink of his sweet tea, he tipped his head in the affirmative. "My relationship with Laurel was an easy one. There's no sense in complicating matters now that it's over."

"I'll take care of everything," Kara promised. "I don't want you or Laurel to have to worry about anything."

"With you at the helm? Never," he offered gently. Then he glanced at his watch. "It's getting late. I'd better go and let you get to bed."

She padded after him in her bare feet when he slid off the stool and headed for the front of the house. He opened the door, then turned to face her, hand still on the brass knob.

"Thanks for keeping me company tonight."

"It was my pleasure," she told him. "And I really am sorry things didn't work out with you and Laurel."

He didn't respond for a second. Instead, his attention seemed to be locked on her lips. She licked them self-consciously, wondering if she had a spot of tea there, or some smeared lipstick from earlier.

"At least I still have you," he murmured in a low voice without lifting his gaze.

Kara didn't know what to make of that. Of the words or his tone.

But she didn't have long to wonder about it, either. One minute he was staring at her, so intently she almost began to fidget. The next, he was moving in, coming closer and closer until his mouth covered hers.

Everything inside of Kara went stock-still as soon as their lips touched. She stopped moving, stopped breathing, stopped thinking.

The kiss was warm and soft and tasted of sweet tea, with a hint of the Scotch he'd consumed earlier. It was everything she'd ever imagined and more. It started out so slow and tentative, just a brush of lips on lips. Then, as though a match had been struck, it was so much more.

Grabbing her by the upper arms, Eli dragged her against him. She could feel the heat of him through the thin silk of her robe, the press of his arousal at her belly.

In all the years she'd dreamed of kissing him, her fantasies had never been like this. Sometimes she'd imagined light, chaste kisses that made her feel like the princess in a fairy tale. Other times, she'd imagined uncontrollable passion that incited him to sweep her into his arms and carry her off to the bedroom à la *Gone with the Wind*.

But this was nothing like either of those scenarios. It was real and raw and made her feel as though her entire being was going up in flames.

She clung to him as the heat radiated through her. His mouth enveloped her, his tongue sweeping inside to claim her in a way she couldn't ever remember experiencing before.

And then it was over. Without warning, he pulled away, took a step back at the same time he set her a step away from him in the opposite direction.

Reality slapped Kara in the face more effectively than a bucket of frigid ice water falling over her head. They were both breathing heavily, chests heaving while they struggled to look anywhere but at each other.

"I should go," he said in little more than a mumble.

The words buzzed in her ears, sounding as though they were coming to her through a very long wind tunnel. Her ears, she realized, were ringing in time with the spinning of her head. The best she could do was nod in agreement as he opened the door and walked out into the night without a backward glance.

Kara stood frozen in place, the events of the past few seconds flashing through her mind. It had been wonderful…it had been terrifying. She wanted it to happen again…she wished it had never happened.

The man of her girlhood dreams—oh, who was she kidding?—her girlhood *and* womanly dreams…had just kissed her half-senseless. And all she could feel was horrendous guilt over the fact that he was her sister's only very recent *ex*-fiancé.

Eli took the long way home. The "long way" being three loops around Kara's block on foot before finally making his way to his car and back to his apartment. The same dark, empty apartment he hadn't wanted to return to earlier.

He didn't particularly want to return there now, but it wasn't as though he had much choice unless he wanted to spend the night in one of his own equally dark and empty hotel rooms.

He'd seriously considered his options during his extended walk, though. Part of him had wanted to lope back up Kara's front steps, pound on the door until she opened it, and burst inside, sweeping her into his arms and upstairs to her bedroom. The other part—the part that ruled his head rather than his libido—wondered how the hell he could kiss his former fiancée's sister like a house afire on the very same day his engagement had been called off.

How he could be lusting after her even now.

Had he ever felt this way after kissing Laurel? He didn't think so. Or at least, he didn't remember so.

All of the kisses with Laurel that he could remember had been fairly chaste…just like the entire rest of their relationship. They had been a lovely, upstanding couple. From the outside, they had probably looked perfectly prim and proper, candidates for gracing the cover of *Garden & Gun*'s "Who's Who of Charleston" edition.

Inside, however, there had been no passion. Respect and friendship, certainly—and that wasn't about to change, regardless of Laurel's decision to call things off.

But until he'd kissed Kara—and he still didn't know what in blue blazes had prompted him to do it—he hadn't realized just how lacking in passion his relationship with Laurel had been. Kissing Kara had been like touching a live wire. It had scorched him from his lips to the top of his head and all the way back down to his toes. He couldn't recall ever having such an intense reaction to kissing a woman…or if he had, she'd blown the memory straight out of his brain.

The question was: what the *hell* was he going to do about it?

The smart thing would be to go home, take a shower, climb into bed, and forget that the kiss had ever happened.

The blood still pounding in his head and through his veins—not to mention lower extremities—with the force of molten lava told him that was clearly going to be an impossibility.

Which put him back at square one with *what the hell was he going to do about this sudden, powerful attraction to Kara Kincaid?*

Four

Kara hadn't slept a wink the night before. How could she after that kiss? It had been as though she had two invisible demons sitting on either shoulder, pulling her in opposite directions like a wishbone.

Those little invisible entities hadn't taken the forms of the typical devil and angel, though. Oh, no. Instead, they'd very clearly sported the faces of Eli and Laurel.

Eli smiling, winking, being his usual charming self, doing his best to smooth-talk her into another soul-shattering kiss with that smooth Southern drawl. (Just because she shared that accent didn't mean she couldn't still be affected by it.)

And then Laurel on the other side, frowning, her eyes filled with hurt, asking, *Why, Kara? How could you do this to me... your very own* sister?

No, she didn't sleep a wink with *that* preying on her conscience.

So here she was, up at the crack of dawn. Which wasn't all that unusual—a lot of her days began before the sun started its slow climb into the sky.

Normally, however, she was functioning with eight solid hours of sleep to keep her upright. Also normally, she would be dressed for work, and either already in her office at the front of the house or on her way to her first appointment.

But today was far from normal. Instead of continuing to plan her sister's wedding, she was supposed to be in the process of dismantling it. Instead of being dressed in a stylish, professional skirt and blouse, she was in her bare feet, wearing one of her favorite light-as-air sundresses covered in giant orange poppies, with a thick, neck-to-knee apron over that. It was hot pink, with white lace along the top and at both of the pockets in the center, and had *Everyone has their price...mine is chocolate* stitched beside a delicious-looking pile of chocolates.

Like a lot of women raised in the South, when the going got tough, the tough got cooking. Or baking, as the case may be.

Even growing up as she had, in a house filled with servants—or household help, as was probably the more politically correct term these days—any time her mother had felt undue stress, she'd ended up in the kitchen, up to her elbows in flour with a rolling pin in her hand. Sometimes she'd baked her weight in biscuits. Other times she'd fried enough chicken to feed the entire Confederate army. And still others, she'd made so many cookies all of the Kincaid children had been sent to school the next day with bags enough to become homeroom heroes.

Elizabeth had also taught each of her girls to cook—and the boys, too, if they were willing to learn. At least enough that they wouldn't starve if they were ever left to their own devices.

Thanks to her mother's talented instruction, Kara made a mean honey-glazed ham and created desserts so yummy that she'd briefly considered opening her own bakery before deciding to go into event planning instead. Mainly because she was only motivated to bake when she was emotional, for some reason—angry, sad, nervous...or in this case, guilty and confused. And what kind of bakery could stay open if the owner baked only when she was in the mood?

As it was, she didn't know what she was going to do with the butter pecan cookies that even now were beginning to cool on her marble countertop. All she knew was that she needed to keep busy. Needed the precision of measurements, the therapeutic act of mixing, and the repetitive movements of dropping dough onto cookie sheets, then sliding them off with a spatula when they were done.

At exactly 8:15 a.m., the phone rang. It startled her. This was her personal line, not the business line in her office, and she rarely got personal calls so early in the morning...unless something was wrong. And considering her family's current troubles, something could indeed be wrong.

Her stomach clenched and her fingers tightened inside her oven mitt as she set another cookie sheet on top of the stove. Lord, what now? Her father had been murdered, her mother had been arrested for his death, her sister had called off her wedding... What more could happen that hadn't already—fires, floods, pestilence?

The minute the thought crossed her mind, she shook herself and wished she could call it back. There was no better way to jinx something than to ask that exact question, and her family sure as all get-out didn't need any more jinxes falling on them.

Shedding the oven mitt and saying a quick prayer that this was *not* going to be more bad news, she picked up the cordless receiver from its cradle and hit the talk button.

"Hello?"

"Kara, hon, it's Penelope from Eli's office."

The familiar voice sang over the line, lifting the cloud of foreboding that had begun to weigh her down. She blew out a breath even as she wondered why Eli's assistant was calling her on her personal line. They'd had plenty of interaction over the past few months, setting up meetings to go over wedding plans, but that had always been on her business line.

"Hello, Penelope. How are you?"

"Just fine, sweetie. How about you?"

"Fine," she replied by rote.

"Mr. Houghton asked me to call you at home and set up an appointment for this afternoon. Are you available?"

Kara's heartbeat sped up and her lungs began to burn until she realized she'd stopped breathing. Inhaling quickly, she told herself to stop being such a ninny and asked, "Do you know why he wants to meet?"

A short pause. "I just assumed it was more to do with the wedding. Why—are you busy today?"

It was a simple enough question, but Kara heard the eager curiosity underlying the words.

"No, no," she answered before Penelope became any more suspicious than she already was.

Eli obviously hadn't said anything about his broken engagement, and Kara wasn't about to be the one to start the Charleston rumor mill churning. Penelope was a dedicated employee, but this was the South—gossip was practically a sporting event.

"I'll be happy to meet with him whenever he likes," she added. He probably just wanted to get together to discuss the cancellations and make sure she covered all the details.

And if he could act as though nothing untoward happened last night, so could she.

The doorbell rang forty minutes later, a full hour earlier than she'd been expecting. With a jolt of panic, Kara dropped the last of her dirty utensils in the dishwasher and took a quick glance around the kitchen to make sure it didn't look like a natural disaster had struck.

The problem with baking, she grumbled silently on her way to the front door, was that once you started, you couldn't stop. Not unless you wanted everything ruined and gone to waste.

So even though she'd told Penelope she was at Eli's disposal and agreed to meet with him at 10 a.m., as soon as she'd hung up the phone, she'd had to go right back to sliding cookies hot from the oven onto cooling racks, spooning fresh batter onto empty sheets, and repeating until she'd run out. She'd done it all as quickly as humanly possible, but the laws of physics only allowed these things to move so fast.

Which left her not much time to clean up, ditch the apron, change her clothes and refresh her hair and makeup. If Eli had shown up as scheduled instead of devilishly early, she might actually have made it. As it was, she was hoping against hope that someone else was at the door. A neighbor asking to borrow sugar—something she was low on, thanks to her early-morning baking binge—or maybe one of her brothers needing a favor... or wanting to grab a handful of cookies, since they seemed capable of smelling the scents of her kitchen from a mile away.

Wiping her hands on her apron, she yanked open the door... and released a sigh of resignation. Of course.

"Good morning, Eli," she said, stepping back to invite him inside. "You're early."

He shot her a dazzling smile. "What can I say? I was eager to see you again."

Caterpillars broke through their cocoons and turned into butterflies inside her stomach. So much for pretending last night hadn't happened.

"Actually, I have meetings all afternoon and wanted things hammered out with you before I get distracted. I hope you don't mind."

She asked, "What things did you have in mind?"

Rather than answering, he tipped his head to the side and sniffed. "Do I smell pie?"

"Cookies, actually," she corrected.

He lifted one brow and gave her a look.

Her lips twitched as she struggled not to grin. "Would you like some?"

"Yes, please," he said with enthusiasm, actually clapping his hands and rubbing them together.

"Come on." Reaching behind her, she loosened the ties of her apron as she led him back to the kitchen. Once they arrived, she slipped it over her head and folded it to set on one of the stools beside the center island.

"You must have gotten up awfully early to do all this," he remarked, taking in the dozens upon dozens of cookies covering every flat surface in the room.

She ignored that, instead busying herself by collecting a small plate and filling it with cookies, then setting it on the counter in front of him. He was sitting in the same spot as last night, looking infinitely comfortable. As though he was used to lounging around in her kitchen. As though he belonged there.

Lifting a cookie halfway to his mouth, he paused to study it.

"Butter pecan," she supplied a scant second before he took a bite and let out a long, appreciative moan.

Eli wasn't new to her baking skills. They'd grown up together, and he'd spent enough time with her family as an adult that he'd been the recipient of plenty of both her and her mother's culinary creations.

But for some reason, having him here with her—just the two of them, in her home, in her oven-heated kitchen—felt more… intimate than any of the other times he'd sat across from her, eating her cookies.

Clearing her throat in an attempt to shake off the uncomfortable tingle building beneath her skin, she asked, "Would you like something to drink with those? I know you're not overly fond of tea, but maybe a cup of coffee or…" She trailed off, running a mental inventory of her refrigerator.

"Got any milk?"

It was her turn to raise a brow. Milk was certainly the perfect choice of drink to go with a plate of fresh-from-the-oven cookies, but for some reason, she hadn't expected such a request from a man like Eli, who just last night had shown up on her doorstep filled with double malt Scotch.

"Of course," she told him, moving first to the cupboard, then the refrigerator.

She poured them each a glass before hopping up on her stool and snatching a cookie for herself. Eli had already chomped through three of the rich, fattening blobs, but Kara rarely did more than sample her own treats. After all, she knew what went into them and how many calories she would be forced to burn off at the gym if she overindulged.

"So," she prompted, after they'd both spent a few minutes chewing and washing the crumbs down with sips of cold milk. "What is it you wanted to discuss? Concerns about the dissolution of the wedding plans?"

She cringed inwardly the moment the words were out of her mouth. How could she be so thoughtless? Why hadn't she kept her stupid mouth shut?

It was too early to be bringing up the called-off marriage vows in such a callous fashion. Eli had to be stinging still from Laurel's rejection. She could have just as easily sat here while they enjoyed their cookies and let him get to his reason for dropping by in his own sweet time.

Eli, however, didn't seem fazed. He finished off the cookie in his hand, washed it down with a gulp of milk, and then wiped his mouth with the napkin she'd provided, before speaking.

"You said you could handle all of that, so unless you need me for something, I'd rather leave everything to you."

"All right," Kara replied carefully. If he didn't need to talk to her about that, then what *did* he need to talk to her about?

Please not the kiss...please not the kiss...please not the kiss...

"I'm not sure I've mentioned before how impressed I was with your work on the wedding plans."

He said it in the same tone of voice he might compliment her cooking. No hint of pain or resentment or happiness.

"You're very efficient and have great taste."

"Thank you," she responded, still choosing her words carefully.

"Which got me to thinking that Houghton Hotels and Resorts might benefit from your expertise."

All right, Kara thought slowly, that was unexpected. But aloud, she said, "How so?"

"We do a lot of high-end events—weddings, anniversaries, birthday parties, bar mitzvahs—especially at the Ocean Breezes location. The one on Seabrook Island," he clarified, as though she wasn't already more than familiar with every one of his half-dozen-and-growing hotels.

"At the moment, we have a resort employee handling that sort of thing, but I think we could do an even better job and become even more of a go-to site for large, upscale special occasions if we had a professional on board who really knew what she was doing, and whose only job was to plan and oversee those events."

Seconds passed while she absorbed his statement and tried to make sense of it. "Are you asking me to give up Prestige Events and work for you instead?"

He shook his head, sneaking another cookie. "Of course not. Prestige is your baby, I understand that. But if you'd be willing to branch out a bit, maybe sub-contract some work, I really think I could use your input."

She let another beat or two go by. "What, exactly, are you asking me to do?"

"Come with me to Ocean Breezes for a few days," he said casually around half a bite of butter pecan. "I know the wedding was the only project on your agenda for the next few weeks, so now that it's been called off, I assume you're free. With the exception of canceling everything, of course, but since we've got telephones and fax machines at the Seabrook Island location, that shouldn't be a problem."

"And what would I do once I got there?" she asked, amazed at how calm she sounded when inside she felt as though a Fourth of July parade was marching up and down her spine. She tingled all over, torn between the excitement of an offer that could lead to some *very* lucrative business for her firm, and the trepidation of being forced to—getting to?—spend more time in Eli's presence.

"Look around. Talk to the woman I've got in charge of special events for the resort at the moment. Review some of our past events to see what we're doing right, and what we might be doing wrong."

"And then...?" she prompted.

Downing the last of his milk, he set the empty glass on the countertop with a clink. "And then we'll talk. You can give me your honest assessment of how we've been handling things. I suspect I'll want to discuss the possibility of contracting Prestige Events for a bit of work in the future, but I'm happy to take things a step at a time."

"So you just want me to visit the resort with you, offer my planning expertise." She made it a statement, but it was really a question.

"Exactly."

He flashed her a dazzling smile, one not dotted with a single crumb, while she would probably look like Cookie Monster if she smiled that wide.

"Look at it this way," he added when she kept her mouth firmly closed. "If it ends up being a waste of time, business-wise, at least you got a nice, all-expenses-paid weekend get-away out of it."

She thought that over for a minute, weighing all of the pros and cons in her head—or at least the ones she could fathom at that particular moment.

Pro: This was Eli, a man she'd known since adolescence and *knew* she could trust. He might be an accomplished business-man and drive a hard bargain when it came to negotiations, but he would never cheat or try to take advantage of her.

Con: This was Eli, the man she'd had half a crush on for three-quarters of her life, and who had kissed her last night like he meant it.

Pro: Being asked to consult for one of Eli's multi-million-dollar hotels—any of them, but the uber-luxurious Seabrook Island location, especially—was a huge opportunity, profes-sionally speaking.

Con: Her sister had just broken up with him the day before. Both the kiss last night and his offer today were likely responses to being jilted by his fiancée only a month before they were scheduled to exchange vows.

Pro: Getting out of town for a few days and keeping his mind on business would probably be one of the best ways for him to avoid a lot of the gossip, and help him heal from the breakup with Laurel. Not that he would ever admit he was suffering or needed time to recover.

Con: Going away with Eli—regardless of the fact that it would be business-only—might not look good to outside observers. *Sister of bride-to-be runs off with groom-to-be the week after wedding is called off...* It was a headline waiting to happen.

And how would Laurel feel about her doing such a thing? Would she understand that Kara was simply exploring a golden business opportunity, or would she see it as a personal betrayal by her very own sister?

It was like being on a seesaw—back and forth, good and bad.

Tipping her head to the side, she studied him, trying not to let his handsome face or cappuccino-brown eyes influence her decision.

"All expenses paid, hmm?" she murmured.

"Yep."

"That's an awfully tempting offer."

"Wait until you get there. You'll think you've died and gone to paradise."

He wiggled his brows, making her chuckle in spite of her determination not to.

"I'd like to say yes," she told him, "but think I should sleep on it at least one night. And...I'm sorry," she said after a slight hesitation, "but I need to talk to Laurel about it first. With everything that's going on right now, I wouldn't feel comfortable taking off unless she and the rest of my family are okay with me being gone."

"Of course," he responded quickly, pushing back from the countertop and climbing to his feet. "Take as long as you need…as long as you don't take too long," he added with a wink.

She followed his lead, trailing him out of the kitchen.

"If you decide you want to go, we can leave as early as Friday morning," he said as they reached the front door. Just like the night before, he turned with his hand on the knob.

At the memory of that, and of what had come next, Kara tensed, her nerve endings going on high alert. She hoped to heaven he didn't try to kiss her again…and at the same time wished he would.

"And if I decide I don't?" she ventured to ask.

He cast her a glance that clearly said he didn't expect to be turned down, no matter how long she took to make up her mind.

"Then I'll hie you away to one of HHR's closer locations instead," he said simply.

A shiver tightened her belly and squeezed her throat. She knew he was talking business, but he made it sound for all the world like an intimate proposition. Like a visit to one of his hotels would be spent in a penthouse suite, burning up the five-thousand-thread-count Egyptian cotton sheets rather than touring the location and offering advice for improving their event-hosting skills.

As though he could read her mind and knew exactly what was making her temperature rise, one corner of his mouth lifted.

"Thanks for the cookies," he murmured. "Call me when you decide what you want to do."

And then he was gone, slipping out the door and leaving her alone in her foyer. *Without* attempting to kiss her again.

Five

Eli was in the middle of reviewing a handful of renewal contracts with some of his hotels' vendors when his receptionist buzzed.

"Kara Kincaid on line three," she said, then clicked off without waiting for a response.

Taking his time, he glanced at his watch.

Four hours. That was fast. He hadn't expected to hear from her until at least tomorrow, given her comment that she needed to "sleep on it."

Of course, he didn't know that she was calling to accept his offer. She could just as easily be calling to give him a short and sweet rejection.

Hoping that wasn't the case, he picked up the receiver and brought it to his ear.

"Hello, darlin'," he greeted her in his—he hoped—friendliest and most cajoling voice.

It must have caught her off guard because the only thing he heard for the count of ten was silence.

"If you're still interested in having me go to Seabrook Island with you," she said slowly, as though she were weighing her words carefully, "then I accept your offer."

"Excellent," he drawled, trying not to let his mouth curve into a Cheshire-cat smile and failing miserably. "I'll pick you up at eight o'clock Friday morning. Will that work?"

"That will be fine," she replied primly.

"Pack for the beach," he told her in a low, just-this-side-of-seductive tone. "See you then."

He hung up before she could reply and while his luck was still running strong.

He pulled up in front of her row house bright and early Friday morning, five minutes before eight. Normally when he visited his resort on Seabrook Island, he drove his BMW Z4 Roadster convertible. It was a sexier, sportier vehicle, and he enjoyed the sting of the open air as he tooled down the expressway, then past burgeoning marshes and canopies of oak and cypress trees as he got closer to the magnificence of the Atlantic Ocean.

But this time, because he wanted to appear harmless and lull Kara into a false sense of security, he was driving the Mercedes-Benz. Safe, comfortable, subtly impressive—it should create the perfect impression for Step One of Operation Win Over Kara Kincaid.

Amazing, he thought, that only two days after being dumped by his fiancée, he was preparing a systematic seduction of her sister. It sounded shameless, even in his own mind, and he was sure there would be plenty of folks within Charleston society who would whisper and shake accusing fingers behind his back.

Not that he gave a tinker's damn. They could say anything they wanted to about him, the same as they had when he was a scraggly foster kid newly moved in with the Youngs—one of the wealthiest families in Charleston, with blood that was very blue and could probably be traced back to the Mayflower.

Boy, he'd had a chip on his shoulder back then. He'd been bitter and angry about the hand life had dealt him, putting on a tough front to keep from being hurt again. He'd been scared, too, never knowing when another shoe might fall or what might be waiting around the next corner.

But having the Youngs take him in, treat him like their own, and not give up on him no matter what, the way so many other foster families had in the past, had taught him self-assurance. They had raised him to be confident in his own thoughts and decisions, regardless of others' opinions.

He wanted Kara Kincaid, and just as he'd gone after building his multi-million-dollar enterprise with his head down, full steam ahead, he intended to go after her.

Until this week, he'd thought he had his life together, both personally and professionally. It was startling to realize how far off-base he'd been in that assessment.

He'd thought he was happy with Laurel—and would be for the next fifty years. Now, the only woman on his mind, the only woman he could fathom spending the rest of his life with, was Kara.

He'd been dating the wrong sister. Planned to marry the wrong sister. Thank God Laurel had put a halt to things when she did, otherwise they both might have made the biggest mistake of their lives.

Cutting the engine, he stepped out of the car and pocketed the keys. At this time of morning, most of the residents on Kara's street had already left for work, but a few people were out walking their dogs or tending their flowers.

Stopping at the curb, he waited for an older woman to pass, offering her a polite smile. She was obviously out for her daily walk, dressed in a hot pink tracksuit with matching head and wristbands.

She was also eyeing him like the captain of the Neighborhood Watch. He wouldn't be surprised if she hit the corner, turned around and came back to see if he was welcome on Kara's doorstep or deserving of a call to the police.

Biting back a chuckle, he crossed the sidewalk and strode to the front of Kara's house, using the antiqued brass knocker to give a couple good raps. Moments later, Kara opened the door.

Her hair was down, falling around her face and shoulders in fat chestnut waves instead of pulled back into a loose bun or intricate twist the way she normally wore it when she worked. Her glasses were also missing, another habit he'd noticed more often than not when she was on personal time and didn't need to look quite as pulled-together and professional.

Her clothes, too, were more casual and beach-worthy, just as he'd advised. She wore a short-sleeve floral blouse made of some sort of flowy, lightweight material, with a lime-green skirt and sexy but comfortable sandals on her feet.

Minimum jewelry—just a small gold cross necklace and gold hoops at her ears. It was understated, but classy and totally Kara. He liked it.

But as beautiful as she looked, she also looked nervous. Her eyes were hooded, her mouth crooked as she nibbled on the inside corner of her lower lip, and he couldn't help but notice the constant, fidgety movements of the hand hanging at her side.

Eli almost felt sorry for her. He'd tried hard not to make her uncomfortable with his invitation to visit his resort. He'd avoided touching her or getting too close, and he'd very pointedly *not* mentioned the kiss they'd shared, even though it was practically the *only* thing he'd been able to think about since.

The smell of her, the taste of her, the feel of her soft body pressed ever so lightly against his own... Just the memory of that short kiss had the power to heat his blood all over again.

He was hoping for an encore very, very soon, but couldn't let Kara know that was his number one priority. If he did, she was likely to get spooked and run all the way back to Charleston.

Not that Eli could blame her. He suspected she was just as interested in him as he was in her, but the circumstances were far from ideal.

A week ago, he'd been on the fast track to becoming her brother-in-law. Now, he had his sights set firmly on her. He could just imagine the checklist she would come up with of all the reasons they should avoid each other like the bubonic plague.

Which meant he had only the weekend to convince her otherwise. To convince her that the attraction humming between them was worth exploring, regardless of the gossip it was likely to create.

Gossip died down...eventually. But he wasn't sure his yearning for her would. Or that, if he let her go, he would ever get another chance at something like this. A chance to be with a woman he thought might be The One.

It was a bold move for him. Deciding to propose to Laurel had taken months of careful consideration. He'd analyzed every aspect of their relationship—past, present and possible future—before concluding that she was a prudent choice to become his wife. And that only after taking even longer to decide he wanted a wife at all.

For the past few years, he'd felt as though something was missing from his life. He had a good, solid family now, and had long ago come to terms with his past and childhood origins. His business was booming, too, so there were no holes there.

The same couldn't be said about his personal life, however. In that respect, he had been sadly lacking.

Which was why, after mulling it over, he'd decided settling down and starting a family was the wisest course of action. It had taken quite a while longer to narrow down his list of possible brides-to-be and land on Laurel Kincaid.

She'd seemed so perfect. On paper, anyway.

Little had he realized how overrated on-paper perfection was.

Laurel was a lovely woman, inside and out. She would be a wonderful wife for some man someday. Of that, Eli had no doubt. But that didn't mean she was the perfect wife for him.

No, he suspected that role might be better suited to Laurel's sister. Which was awkward, to be sure—but not impossible.

He only hoped he could convince Kara to be as open-minded as he was feeling these days. But in order to do that, he had to start slow and do his best not to let her know he had more than simply business in mind for their weekend away.

"Good morning," he greeted her, keeping things casual, upbeat. He was still on the other side of the threshold, one hand resting against the doorjamb. "Ready to go?"

She nibbled the inside of her bottom lip a minute longer, both corners of her mouth drawn down in a worried frown.

"Are you sure this is a good idea?" she asked. "With everything that's going on, maybe I shouldn't be leaving town. Especially with you."

He slapped a hand over his heart, pretending to be wounded. "Why, darlin', I do believe you've hurt my feelings."

She chuckled at that, knowing darn well he was kidding.

"Fine," she told him, reaching for the handle of one of the overnight bags at her feet. There were three in varying sizes and shapes, all part of a matching designer set. She thrust the largest at him before picking up the other two and stepping outside, shutting and locking the door behind her.

"But if anything happens and I can't be here with my family when they need me, I'm blaming you."

"It's just Seabrook Island," he reminded her as they headed for his car and he popped the trunk to load her bags. "A single phone call from your family, and I can have you back to Charleston within the hour. Less, if you want me to put a helicopter on standby."

She shot him a withering glare before ducking into the passenger seat. "That won't be necessary."

He grinned back at her, then slammed the door and walked around to the driver's side. They drove in relative silence until they hit the expressway before broaching a subject he'd been curious about ever since she'd first called to accept his invitation-slash-job offer.

"I take it Laurel was okay with you running off with me for the weekend," he said, keeping his tone light and just this side of flippant.

For a moment, she seemed to hesitate, then she gave a short nod. Readjusting her seatbelt, she turned slightly to face more in his direction.

"She said she didn't mind at all. She even claimed to think that my working with you was a good idea."

He couldn't resist a tiny smirk. "Told you so."

"She sounded distracted, though," Kara added without rising to the bait. "I don't know if it's Daddy's death and Mama being blamed for it, or calling off the wedding to you, or something else altogether, but she hasn't been herself lately."

"You've both got a lot on your minds these days. Anyone in your situation would."

Kara tipped her head to one side, whether in agreement or simply in thought, he wasn't sure.

"Laurel and Mama were supposed to travel next month before the wedding. Mama can't go, of course, now that she's being accused of Daddy's murder, but she doesn't want Laurel to cancel the trip. I think there's a part of Laurel that still wants to go, if only to get away from all the craziness here at home. But there's another part of her that will feel guilty if she goes, because it will be like abandoning Mama or running off when the family needs her most."

"Sort of like you running off with me this weekend."

Eli purposely let his words hint at a double entendre, curious to see what Kara's response might be. Would she immediately deny that they were "running off" or rush to clarify that it wasn't *that* kind of trip? Or would she let it slide, silently acknowledging that it may indeed turn out to be *that* kind of trip?

To his surprise and delight, she let it slide.

"Yes. I told her she should go. It sounds selfish, but I think she could use the time away. She'll come back with a clearer head, feeling more refreshed. And just like you said about me this weekend, if anything comes up that she needs to be here for, she can get home in a matter of hours."

"Exactly," he agreed, reaching over to take her hand. He twined their fingers together, pleased when she didn't try to stop him. "So now that you believe getting out of town for a few days is a good idea for your sister, maybe you'll start to believe it's a good idea for yourself, too."

She chuckled, her fingers tightening around his. Whether it was accidental or deliberate, however, he wasn't sure.

"I guess I have to, otherwise I risk being a hypocrite, don't I?"

"You certainly do," he agreed.

"Hmm," she murmured. "I think I'm beginning to learn what makes you such a successful entrepreneur. You're a tough negotiator."

"Damn straight."

Though she didn't know the half of it. But by the end of the weekend, she very well might. He would beg, borrow or steal to convince her to launch into a steamy, clandestine affair with him.

"Of course, it helps that I'm simply stating the obvious."

"Arrogant, too," she quipped. "How lucky that I get to spend the entire weekend with Mr. Know-it-All."

"You love me, and you know it," he shot back, bringing her hand to his mouth and pressing a quick kiss to her knuckles.

Eli wasn't certain why he was pushing her so far so soon, when he'd been determined to be a perfect gentleman until they were comfortably settled at Ocean Breezes. But after dropping the first hint that there might be more to their relationship than she wanted to admit and not having her deny it, he felt compelled to press again.

Both his words—the *L* word, coupled with the declaration that she had feelings for him—and the intimacy of the kiss to her hand were designed to test her boundaries. Would she pull away? Would she correct him? Would she laugh it off or concede that, yes, she did love him, but only as a friend?

Oh, how that one would hurt. Because they *were* friends, but he wanted them to be more. And everybody knew that once a woman soundly relegated a man to the "friend" column, he had a better chance of sprouting wings and flying to the moon than ever making it even close to the "potential lover" category.

He didn't expect her to jump across the console and molest him while he was driving, but when she untangled their fingers and slowly pulled her hand away to rest in her lap, he caught his breath. Anticipating the worst and wishing he'd kept his damn mouth shut.

"I do love you," she said quietly.

So quietly, he barely heard her. When he chanced a quick glance in her direction, he found her no longer leaning toward him, but sitting up straight, staring ahead out the windshield.

"You're one of my dearest friends."

Bum-bum-BUM. The impending doom score from every movie he'd ever seen reverberated through his head.

Well, there it was. The kiss of death. A minute ago, he'd been pulsing with anticipation of the weekend to come. Now, he was almost sick with dread and wondering how the hell he was going to get through the next three days.

"I don't think I've ever thanked you for all your support when Daddy first died. Being there for me, day or night."

He'd been one of the first callers to show up at the Kincaid Mansion as soon as he heard about Reginald's untimely death. It had been a suspected suicide then, which had left the family reeling. But then, finding out later that it was murder hadn't been much better.

He liked to think he'd been there to support all of the Kincaids, doing whatever he could to help them in their time of need. But after the reading of the will, when each of Reginald's children had gone home with a letter written specifically to them by their father, Kara had been the one to call him, sobbing.

There hadn't been anything particularly pertinent in her letter. Kara wasn't greatly involved in the family businesses, so there were no instructions on how to run the Kincaid Group or last requests for something Reginald wanted to see done. It was simply a father reaching out to his daughter one final time, telling her how much he loved her.

Eli had stayed on the phone with her well into the night, saying what he could to comfort her, listening to her voice her grief and share special memories of her father that no one else—not even her brothers and sisters, in many cases—possessed. And he'd been happy to do it, grateful that there was *something* he could do for her at a time when he felt pretty damn helpless otherwise.

"Any time," he said now. "You know that."

"I do," she said in barely a whisper. "I do know that."

They were the last words spoken between them all the way to Seabrook Island.

Six

This was a mistake.

At a time when she should be taking in the view, enjoying a leisurely drive to a gorgeous ocean resort, Kara was a bundle of nerves, and all she could think was that agreeing to take off with Eli, even for business purposes, had been a terrible mistake.

How in the name of heaven was she supposed to get through the weekend with him, feeling as she did right now?

From the moment he'd dropped that bomb—*you love me and you know it*—her heart had kicked up like an electric power generator and had been chugging along at full speed.

She did love him, just as she'd admitted. But while she'd focused on their friendship, deep down she was afraid she wanted more than that. Not in some ethereal, childhood fantasy, dream lover way, but in a very solid, realistic, forever kind of way.

It couldn't happen, of course. Despite the kiss they'd shared—which was likely the combined result of stress from a broken engagement, exhaustion from the late hour and too many scotches with dinner—Kara knew he didn't really have *those kinds* of feelings for her.

He liked her well enough, felt warmly toward her because of their shared childhood and appreciated her support after Laurel had dumped him. But he didn't *want her*-want her. Didn't want to toss her on the bed, tear her clothes off and have his wicked way with her.

She shivered at the very thought, because that's exactly what she'd like him to do.

Then she thought of her sister and felt her face flush with the sting of shame.

How could she even be *considering* such things about her sister's former fiancé? How would Laurel feel if she knew Kara was lusting after Eli, and had since she was a teenager?

The most likely answer—that even if Laurel wasn't ready to marry him herself didn't mean she was willing to hand him over to her own baby sister on a silver platter—was the biggest reason this weekend *was a huge mistake*.

They were on Seabrook Island now, drawing closer and closer to his resort, and Kara didn't have a clue what she was going to do once they arrived. Would she be able to tamp down her emotions and act as though nothing was wrong? As though they were nothing more than friends doing a bit of mutually beneficial business? Or would she spend the weekend walking on pins and needles, teetering on the ragged edge of a panic attack?

Crushed shells crunched beneath the Mercedes's tires as they traversed the curving drive leading to the front of the seaside resort. She'd been to Ocean Breezes once before, for the grand opening and ribbon-cutting ceremony. She'd been so proud of Eli that day—as proud as he'd been of his new "baby." Ocean Breezes wasn't just a hotel, after all, which all of his other ventures had been up to that point, but a full-blown resort with everything a guest could possibly want in an island getaway.

A private beach, private golf course, on-site spa and in-room spa treatments. Exclusive shops and a high-end salon right on the premises. Restaurants to die for. And, of course, all the amenities for those once-in-a-lifetime special events she would be consulting on: weddings, anniversaries, bridal and engagement parties, even the occasional sweet sixteen celebration.

She couldn't wait to experience the true luxury she knew stood beyond the front doors.

Eli pulled beneath the wide portico shading the main entrance, and a second later a valet was rounding the hood of the car to open her door for her. The young man was dressed in black slacks, white button-down shirt and a maroon vest with the Ocean Breezes logo emblazoned on the breast pocket. He greeted her with a wide smile, waiting for her to step out before moving again to Eli's side of the car.

"Welcome back, Mr. Houghton. It's a pleasure to see you again."

"Thank you, Robert," Eli returned, passing the boy his keys, along with a folded bill of what looked to be a high denomination as a tip.

At the same time, another Breezes employee removed their luggage from the trunk, placing it on a wheeled, brass-plated cart. When that was done, Eli tipped him, too.

"They all go to my private suites," he told the other young man in a low voice. "And see that strawberries and a bottle of champagne are delivered there, as well. Thank you, Julio."

Kara was more than impressed that he knew his staff by name. She wondered if that was true of all of his hotel and resort locations, considering how many he owned now and how many individuals he must retain at each.

As the car rolled away in one direction and their luggage in another, Eli came to her side, taking her arm and tucking it securely within his own. He began leading her through the glass doors and into the lobby, their heels clicking on the glistening marble floor.

"Strawberries and champagne?" she murmured, repeating

what she'd overheard, but making it a question rather than a statement.

"To celebrate," he said simply.

"Celebrate what?"

"The start of what I expect to be a very lucrative and successful partnership."

"A thank-you note would have sufficed," she told him flatly.

He chuckled, leaning over to press a quick kiss to her temple. "Don't be silly, darlin'. A woman like you would never be impressed by something so mundane."

"Are you trying to impress me?" she asked.

"Of course," he replied without hesitation. "I always try to impress lovely ladies when I want something from them."

Kara's pulse leapt, her breath catching in her lungs for a brief second. They passed the reception area, Eli nodding to the two doe-eyed young women behind the registration desk, who were practically giggling behind their hands at their rich, attractive boss's very presence, before leading her to the bank of elevators off to one side. He pressed the up arrow and the gleaming silver doors slid open.

She waited until they were inside the car, alone, and he'd used a special key card to unlock the button for his private level before clearing her throat and forcing herself to ask, "What do you want from me?"

The doors slid open once again. "For you to join me for strawberries and champagne," he responded matter-of-factly, stepping out into the entry area of his private quarters.

Kara exited the elevator, but then stood nailed in place, taking in her opulent surroundings. She'd grown up with money, so she was no stranger to luxury. She'd also toured several of the guest rooms, suites and private bungalows on the premises during the grand opening.

But while those spaces were impressive even by luxury resort standards, Eli's was a cut above that. It also didn't look like a typical Ocean Breezes suite; it looked like a personal residence.

Hardwood floors instead of plush carpeting…sheer white curtains billowing with the breeze blowing in from the ocean instead of heavy, light-blocking drapes…a full, nearly gourmet kitchen instead of a kitchenette…and unique, personally chosen furniture instead of cookie-cutter pieces.

From what she could tell from a glimpse through the French doors on the opposite side of the large sitting area, he also had one of the most magnificent views in the entire resort. Possibly the entire island.

"Don't be afraid," he said from halfway across the room. "You can come in. I won't bite."

She moved away from the elevator, taking slow, deliberate steps as she continued to study the intricacies of the suite. Through a set of double doors off to one side of the living and dining area, she spotted an immaculately made-up king-size bed.

Their bags were stacked at its foot, which meant the bellhop must have really hustled to get in and out of the suite before they arrived. Pausing only a few feet from Eli, she kept her eyes locked on that luggage and the wide, wide mattress beyond.

"I never agreed to stay here with you," she told him, still without peeking in his direction. "I thought I would have my own room."

From the corner of her eye, she saw him shrug a single broad, tailored shoulder. "This will be better. Besides, you're not just another resort guest, you're *my* guest, and we'll be working quite a bit this weekend. It will benefit us to be in close proximity."

Being in *close proximity* to Eli was the problem. She was having trouble enough beating her runaway hormones into submission just standing three feet away in an otherwise spacious room.

How was she supposed to stop the images flitting through her brain and turning her insides to mush if they shared a living space for three days and two nights? It didn't sound like much, but considering the fantasies she'd been entertaining ever since he'd murmured "I won't bite," three *minutes* and two *seconds* had become too long an amount of time to be alone with him.

"I'm not sure I'm comfortable with that," she told him truthfully. Of course, she didn't reveal the *why* of it.

He started toward her, and she finally turned to face him. As always when she saw him, a jolt of electricity skittered through her veins, sending shock waves to every extremity.

He was just so darned handsome. She was certain he knew it—the man did own a mirror, after all, and tended to have random women fawning over him day and night—but he never acted as though his model-perfect features and physique made any difference to him.

He didn't act cocky or entitled. He didn't use them to sway people to his advantage. He didn't even—to her knowledge, at any rate—use them to seduce women into one-night stands.

Oh, she was sure he had affairs, and possibly even girlfriends, though she couldn't remember him ever mentioning a serious relationship other than the one he'd had with Laurel. But while just about every red-blooded woman would be willing to throw herself at him before she even knew his name, Kara had never known him to take them up on their offers just for the sake of quick, sweaty sex.

When was the last time *she'd* had quick, sweaty sex? she suddenly wondered. Or any sex at all.

It had been a while, to say the least.

Let's see… She'd dated Bradley pretty seriously back in college, and they'd experimented with each other in ways that could still make her blush. At the time, she'd believed they would get married and live happily ever after. Too bad Bradley had had other ideas—along with every cheerleader on the pep squad.

It had taken her a while to get over Bradley's betrayal, so for a few years, celibacy had been the name of the game. Then she'd met Christian.

She'd had no delusions that Christian was the man of her dreams, but he'd been funny, good-looking and knew how to show her a good time. The sex had been decent, and she'd enjoyed it, knowing everything about Christian was temporary with a capital *T*.

And that was it—her two claims to sexual adventure. The last of which had ended some time ago.

Meanwhile, Eli's last relationship had ended only a handful of *days* ago.

With her sister. Her sister, her sister, her sister. She really needed to remember that.

"I only see one bed," she pointed out, holding his coffee-brown gaze even as she wanted to look away and take a cautionary step backward. "Where, exactly, am I supposed to sleep?"

Lifting a hand, he brushed his fingers over her cheek and into her hair, tucking a loose strand behind one ear. "You worry too much, darlin'. Now stop frettin' so we can enjoy our weekend and get a little work done."

Oh, it was so simple for him. Obviously, he didn't have an entire race of tiny alien creatures tap-dancing on her nerve endings the way she did.

She opened her mouth to argue, but a chime sounded near the elevator. Dropping his hand, Eli moved around her and went to deal with it.

After he pressed a button on the panel beside the elevator, the doors whooshed open to reveal the same bellhop who'd taken their luggage standing behind a cloth-draped room service cart.

"Mr. Houghton," he greeted Eli with a respectful nod.

Eli inclined his head in return, waving an arm to welcome the young man into the suite. He pushed the cart to the center of the sitting room, smiling at Kara as he passed.

"Would you like me to open the champagne for you, sir?"

"No, thank you, Julio. I can handle it."

With that, the young man moved back to the elevator. "Is there anything else I can do for you?" he asked.

"Not right now, thank you."

"Enjoy your stay, sir," Julio said before stepping into the elevator and disappearing from sight.

Eli lifted the champagne bottle from the ice bucket and wrapped it in a pristine white cloth napkin.

The cork fell from the champagne bottle with a small pop, and he picked up one of the crystal flutes and began to pour.

With both flutes now filled with the bubbly, he held one of them out to her. Kara stayed rooted in place for a moment, feeling as torn as Eve must have been when tempted by the serpent.

Oh, she could spot a neatly baited trap when she saw one. *Come closer, my dear. I won't bite.*

She'd heard that before, hadn't she? And from Eli's very own soft, seductive lips. Never mind the wolf's razor-sharp teeth glittering in full view.

And yet she found herself moving forward, feet dragging even as she reached for the champagne he was offering. She lifted the glass only to have him stop her before she could take a drink.

"Ah-ah-ah. Don't forget the best part."

Taking a strawberry from the bowl sitting on the room service cart, he brought the ripe, red fruit to her lips. She hesitated for a second, desire battling her better judgment...until desire won out.

Opening her mouth, she allowed him to slip the tip of the strawberry inside, then bit down, letting the tart juices coat her tongue and drip down her throat. She was having trouble chewing, though, and when Eli put the same berry to his own lips, taking an even larger, more succulent bite...well, swallowing became all but impossible.

Of course, he didn't seem to be having nearly the same difficulties. He chewed his strawberry with gusto and just before swallowing, took a drink of the champagne, never taking his eyes from her face.

Because she wasn't sure how long she could keep the bite of berry between her teeth without choking to death—especially considering how tight her lungs were growing—she, too, began to chew.

"Now take a sip," he murmured, putting two fingers to the base of her glass and tipping it toward her mouth.

She did as he encouraged, just barely managing to get it down. Not because there was anything wrong with it; on the contrary, both the berry and the bubbly were exquisite.

But being this close to Eli, almost intimately close, in his own personal suite of rooms had her dangerously on edge. Her whole body was tense, vibrating with expectation. Though in expectation of what, she wasn't certain.

As soon as she'd swallowed, Eli was there again, holding another ripe, luscious strawberry up to her mouth, tempting her to give up. To give in.

And, oh, how tempting it was.

But she couldn't let her heart run away with her good sense. Pursing her lips, she shook her head, refusing to let him ply her with any more intoxicating food or wine until she knew exactly where she stood with him.

"What is this, Eli?" she blurted out the minute he lowered his hand, strawberry and all. "You asked me here on business, but this feels like something else. It feels," she said in a much softer voice, "like a seduction."

He lifted one broad shoulder. "Maybe it is," he said in a casual tone. "But then, who says we can't mix a little pleasure with our business?"

Seven

Eli hadn't intended to admit the more wily part of his plan so soon...or at all, frankly...but when Kara asked him point-blank what he was up to, he couldn't bring himself to lie to her.

In retrospect, perhaps the champagne and strawberries hadn't been the best way to open the weekend. They were a bit obvious.

Then again, he was relieved to have the truth of the matter out in the open. He would have felt like a heel if he managed to lure her into bed, only to be forced later to admit that had been his goal all along.

So there it was. His cards were on the table, and now she knew that he had something more in mind for the weekend than simply talking event planning.

How she would react to that admission, however, was yet to be seen. And he knew there were some tall hurdles to jump when it came to making Kara feel comfortable about engaging in an illicit affair with him so soon after his engagement to her sister had ended.

Because she looked like a deer caught in the crosshairs of a hunting rifle, Eli made a quick adjustment to his plans. Returning his champagne and the uneaten strawberry to the room service cart, he took her glass and did the same, then grabbed her hand and tugged her toward the elevator.

"Where are we going?" she asked after he'd pressed the button.

"You'll see."

A moment later, the doors slid open, and he pulled her inside, pressing the button for the lobby. He continued to steer her as they stepped out and crossed the wide-open space. The same two young ladies who had been behind the reception desk when they arrived were still there, and he offered them a polite, if distracted, tip of his head.

Moving across the lobby and down a long, carpeted hallway, he led Kara to the main ballroom where the majority of their large-scale events were held. It was empty at the moment, literally empty of everything but thick carpeting, a centrally located faux wooden dance floor, and an immovable dais along the far wall.

A row of French doors ran the entire length of the room, opening onto a wide verandah that overlooked the ocean. Several yards away, at the end of a grassy, peninsula-shaped bit of land surrounded by a rocky ledge sat a large white gazebo where many a wedding ceremony had taken place.

"So this is our largest, most booked, and *most coveted* area for events," he told her, letting her enter ahead of him. "People enjoy the view and the breeze coming in off the ocean, and both the gazebo and verandah as a backdrop for pictures."

"This is lovely," she said, beginning to wander around, taking in the details from all different angles.

She no longer seemed distracted by the incident in his suite.

"It's perfect for weddings."

"We get a lot of those," he agreed. As well as bookings for the honeymoons that came after.

She moved to the French doors, standing in place for several long minutes. And while Kara studied the landscape, Eli studied her.

She was stunningly beautiful, even turned away from him. Her auburn hair fell around her shoulders in soft, gently curling waves. The lightweight blouse and skirt she was wearing accentuated her feminine curves, from shoulders kept finishing-school-straight to the indent of her waist and back over the flare of her hips. She had great legs, too, whether she was wearing heels or flat sandals like now.

Why did things have to be so damn complicated? he wondered with a silent curse.

He wanted to sidle up to her, stroke the hair away from her neck and kiss the long line of her throat. Spin her around and kiss her senseless. Toss her over his shoulder and carry her back up to his suite, heedless of who might see them.

From there, he wanted to do all manner of wicked, delicious things that would make her forget he'd been engaged to her sister…forget that their being together could be qualified as forbidden…forget everything but the feel of his lips on hers, his naked length pressed to hers, his body moving inside of hers.

The very thought turned him semi-hard and had him shifting uncomfortably from one foot to the other.

But then, he'd always been of the mind that anything worth having was worth working for. If being with Kara were easy, he might not be as interested in her as he was.

Sighing under his breath, he started forward, prepared to open one of the sets of French doors and escort her outside, show her around a portion of the grounds before leading her back to some of the smaller rooms used for lesser events. Only steps from reaching her, he was stopped in his tracks by his name being cried from the opposite doorway.

"Eli!"

He and Kara both turned to see Diane Montgomery swishing her hips as she rushed toward him. Standing on tiptoe, she hugged him a bit too tight, kissed his cheek a bit too close to his mouth.

Long ago, when the plans for Ocean Breezes were first being set in motion, he and Diane had been involved in a short-lived affair. Considering their history, hiring her as the resort's on-site event coordinator probably hadn't been the wisest idea, even if her résumé showed her to be more than qualified for the position.

At the time, she'd been unemployed and somewhat desperate, and she'd done a decent job up to now, even if she did get a little possessive with him and behaved with too much familiarity on occasion.

Bringing Kara in for her professional input on making Ocean Breezes a premiere event location was sure to cause a few bad feelings and a slightly bruised ego for Diane. He only hoped she wouldn't make a scene or do anything to scare off an already skittish Kara.

"The girls at the front desk told me you were here, but I didn't believe them. If you'd let me know you were coming, I could have made sure things were ready for you."

"Everything is fine," he said without intonation, returning her greeting with much less enthusiasm.

Pulling Kara up beside him and keeping her close, Eli introduced the two women. "Kara, this is Diane Montgomery. She's been in charge of events here at the resort since shortly after we opened. Diane, this is Kara Kincaid."

He chose his words carefully, not yet wanting Diane to suspect that Kara might be her replacement, or to imply that she wasn't doing an acceptable job. He also didn't want Kara to know he'd been involved with Diane, even if the relationship was very much past tense.

Kara held her hand out. "Pleased to meet you."

Diane took her hand and gave it a quick shake, but whether Kara noticed it or not, Eli saw the other woman giving her a thorough up-and-down examination. He could almost see the wheels in her head turning, wondering who, exactly, Kara was, what she was doing there and what she meant to Eli.

He certainly wasn't going to enlighten her. Not here, not now…maybe not ever, since who he chose to spend time with was none of her business.

"I was just giving Kara the grand tour," he said. "But I will need to speak to you while I'm here."

Apparently picking up on his all-business tone of voice, Diane glanced at him, then Kara, and back again. The corners of her mouth turned down in a slight frown as she took a step away from them.

"Fine. I'll talk to you later, then."

She turned on her heel and stalked from the ballroom.

"Does she know I'm here to consult on her position?" Kara asked as soon as the other woman was out of sight.

"No," Eli answered simply. Taking her elbow, he led her through one of the unlocked French doors onto the wide verandah.

"I'll tell her when the time comes, if need be. But until you've given me your opinion of the operation here, and how we can improve, I don't see the point in borrowing trouble."

"Fair enough."

"Thank you," he said with a grin, slipping his hand down her arm to link their fingers.

He expected her to pull away, to show the same uneasiness she had back in his suite when he first brought up the idea of turning business into pleasure. Instead, she not only let him twine his hand with hers, but gave him a gentle squeeze in return.

It surprised him how much that small gesture warmed him. Gave him hope that he would be successful in his plan of seduction, after all.

He took her out to the gazebo, which was designed with giant American Beauty roses climbing in a deep blush pink all around the railing and up the posts toward the circular, sloped roof. They didn't go inside, but stood closer to the rocky ledge that overlooked the ocean. A hundred yards below, waves crashed against the shore, sending a salt-tinged breeze up to stir Kara's hair and plaster their clothes to their bodies.

Though the view was breathtaking, Eli didn't normally spend a lot of time on this side of the resort. He didn't like the strong, sometimes violent wind whipping at him, blowing in his face and hair and making it difficult to keep his eyes open.

But experiencing it with Kara suddenly made him see it from a different perspective. Despite the number of weddings they hosted, he'd never considered Ocean Breezes particularly romantic before.

Maybe because he hadn't been paying close enough attention. Or hadn't been standing in the right place, looking out over the churning sea with the right person.

Kara *made* him feel romantic. She made him *want* to order strawberries and champagne, not just because he thought it was a wisely calculated move on his path of seduction, but because she deserved strawberries and champagne, and he wanted to spoil her.

He wanted to take long walks on the beach with her, when the idea of sand in his shoes had never appealed before. He wanted to gaze at her across a candlelit dinner table while they spent three hours paying more attention to one another than their meals.

At that very moment, though, more than anything else, he wanted to reach out and brush the hair away from her face, tip her head back and kiss her.

So he did.

Giving in to temptation, he speared the fingers of his free hand into the hair at her temple, smoothing it back behind her ear, then away from the side of her throat. Leaning down, he pressed his lips to the pulse pounding there. Quickly, erratically. At the same rate his own pulse was pounding in his ears…and lower.

When she didn't pull away, he moved his mouth farther down, to her collar bone, letting his tongue dart out to skim the sharp jut of that sexy protrusion. Then back up, continuing to push her hair out of the way ahead of him so that he could kiss around to her nape, along her shoulder, down toward her shoulder blade.

"Eli."

Her voice came to him in a whisper, one he barely heard over the crashing of the waves below and his own arousal thrumming in his ears.

"Eli," she said again with a reluctant moan.

"Hmm?" he replied without pausing in his exploration of skin that tasted of flowers and honey.

"What are you doing?" she asked on a hush of exhaled breath.

"Kissing you," he murmured against her skin, "what do you think?"

"Why?"

That nearly made him chuckle. It did make him grin.

"Because ever since the kiss we shared in your foyer, I haven't been able to think of a damn thing other than kissing you again," he told her, trailing his mouth over every speck of skin he could reach.

"Because I couldn't resist a minute longer." He nipped the lobe of her ear and traced the line of her jaw.

"Because kissing you is the only thing I can get away with out here without scandalizing guests and starting the rumor mill running at full throttle."

Grasping her chin, he turned her face the last inch to meet his and finally kissed her the way he truly wanted to. His mouth covered hers, grazing her lips, teasing with his tongue until she opened beneath him.

His fingers tunneled into her hair to hold her in place while the kiss deepened. At the same time, he took half a step closer, pressing them together from chest to knee.

A moan rumbled up his throat at the feel of her breasts flattened against him, her legs brushing his, her belly and the apex of her thighs molding to his growing erection through the double layers of her skirt and his trousers. Slipping one hand from the knot of her hair to the small of her back, he tugged her tighter, letting her feel just how much he wanted her. Right here and now, if she would agree…and if they weren't bound to have an audience within a matter of minutes.

Realizing just how true that could be and that they might very well be attracting an audience already, he forced himself to lighten his grip, lighten the pressure of his lips on hers and begin to pull away.

He was breathing hard when they separated. So was she, he was satisfied to notice.

Her lips were swollen a rosy pink from his kisses, her eyes dazed and unfocused. And whether it was the wind blowing in off the Atlantic or the aftereffects of their kiss, she seemed to sway on her feet.

It was the perfect opportunity to sweep her away. Back to his suite and straight into his bed. She was stunned, pliant, and most likely confused about both his actions toward her and her feelings for him.

But as much as he wanted to jump at that excuse, he couldn't. He couldn't take advantage of her. At least not this way. Not yet.

Lifting a hand to her mouth, he used the side of his thumb to wipe away a smudge of lip gloss. He liked it; the smear and bee-stung look made him feel possessive.

Taking a deep breath of salty ocean air to fortify himself, he dropped his arm and clasped one of the limp hands at her side. "Come on," he said, turning on his heel and tugging her with him.

Hurrying to keep up with his long strides, she asked, "Where are we going?"

He slowed his steps and let her catch up, walk beside him rather than running behind. Just because he was frustrated on a massive scale—sexually and otherwise—didn't mean he should take those frustrations out on her.

Pulling her beside him, he wrapped an arm around her

shoulders, pressing a soft kiss to the crown of her head. He held her close, but not too close. Familiarly enough that she would get the point, but not so much that they would garner curious looks from other guests. Or worse yet, his employees.

"I promised you a tour," he told her. "I'm going to give you one before we get distracted and move on to more pleasurable things."

Eight

This was not the weekend Kara had envisioned on the drive down to the island. Even knowing it would be difficult for her to spend so much time in such close contact with Eli, she'd never expected *this*.

How could he suddenly be so interested in her when he hadn't been before? It wasn't just that until a few days ago, he'd been engaged to Laurel. He'd *never* shown an interest in her.

Had he?

She tried to think back on their history together, from middle school on. To all of the times they'd spent together and their countless interactions.

He'd always been kind to her, friendly. But then, he'd been kind and friendly to everyone.

He'd always been there for her, it seemed, through thick and thin. When she'd broken up with her high school boyfriend… when she'd been torn over which college to attend…when her father had died. And in the good times, too—he'd attended her graduations and birthday parties, celebrated with her after the opening of Prestige Events.

But surely he was like that with all his close friends. She imagined he'd been run nearly ragged ever since her father's death. As close as Eli was with the entire Kincaid clan, she was sure each and every one of them had called him at some point since the murder. She was equally sure that he'd spent hours listening to each and every one of them, offering his sympathies and support the same as he had with her.

So that didn't make her particularly special, did it?

Yet when she was with him, she *felt* special.

Of course, her feelings for him had never been in question. She'd always been enamored of him, always had this dreamy, schoolgirl sort of crush on him.

It was *his* feelings for *her* that she wasn't quite as certain of.

Was he toying with her?

At that thought, her heart squeezed almost painfully. If that was the case, she honestly thought she might hurt him. She had carried a torch for him much too long to be seduced and then discarded.

But somehow, she didn't think that could be true. She'd never known Eli to be less than one-hundred-percent honest about anything, and couldn't believe he would ever be so cruel as to make sport of her affections.

But if he wasn't tormenting her, then what was he doing?

It was almost too much to hope that he might truly be interested in her, especially so soon after being engaged to her sister. And yet, here they were.

Kara swallowed hard, doing her best to act as though she was paying attention, while in reality, her mind and pulse were racing.

Eli had shown her the portions of the grounds that were often used for events. He'd taken her through more ballrooms of varying sizes and given her a tour of the kitchens used to cater on-site celebrations.

Now they were headed back to his suite. At least, that's

where she assumed they were going, since there wasn't much more for her to see at the resort that was related to event planning.

He'd promised to schedule an appointment with Diane during their visit so they could sit down and go over dates and figures and paperwork. Kara would need to review how things were currently being run in order to know where there was room for improvement, but she suspected Eli was as reluctant to meet with the other woman as Kara was.

After all, Kara was here to check her work, point out the flaws in her business acumen, and possibly even take over her position as event coordinator for Ocean Breezes. Frankly, Kara wasn't much looking forward to that face-to-face.

At the moment, however, Kara had bigger problems, bigger dilemmas. They were on their way back to Eli's suite of rooms, and she had no idea what she was going to do once they arrived.

Worse, she had no idea what *he* was going to do. Or try to do. Or expect.

She was torn between feeling as though she was walking around in a fairy tale, whisked away for a romantic weekend by a handsome, charming prince…and being swamped by insecurities and guilt.

It was wrong. Giving in to her weakness for Eli was only going to complicate matters. She might be able to get away with it here on Seabrook Island, with no close family to take note of her actions and few prying eyes to watch her every move.

Well, there were prying eyes. The majority of Eli's staff seemed unable to tear their gazes from them any time they passed by. Of course, the fact that Eli had set them up to both stay in his private quarters didn't help matters.

As they reached the bank of elevators, Eli punched the button to call the car.

The elevator doors slid open and they stepped inside. Eli swiped his pass key and punched the button for his private suites.

The doors slid closed, shutting them in together, alone. One minute she was staring at their blurry reflection in the polished silver of the double elevator doors. The next, she was spinning like a top, coming to rest between the hard wall of Eli's broad chest at her front and the cool steel of the doors at her back.

"I can't wait one more minute to do this," he growled.

She opened her mouth to ask *Do what?* but didn't get to voice the first syllable before his mouth crushed down on hers. It took her by surprise, cutting off her oxygen and making her muscles go limp as noodles.

Against her better judgment, when his tongue licked the seam of her lips and he attempted to nudge his way inside, she let him. It was just a kiss, after all. Just one…tiny…kiss.

Somewhere over their heads, a bell dinged. The sound didn't have time to register in her fog-laden brain before the doors behind her slid open and she fell backward.

Eli stumbled after her, catching them both before they ended up in an undignified pile on the foyer floor. Keeping them on their feet, he continued backing her across the entryway until she was once again stopped by a wall. He pinned her there with his body, touching her from collarbones to knee bones.

He kissed her again, not nearly as gently as he had in the elevator. If the kiss in the elevator could be called gentle, which it couldn't. But he didn't wait for her compliance, didn't give her time to adjust or a chance to open her mouth in invitation. He simply took what he wanted.

For long, languid moments, they stood there, tasting, touching. His hands clutched her waist. His erection pressed into her belly. In return, she pawed at his shoulders, her nails kneading him through the material of his suit jacket.

When he released her mouth, she gasped. Then, while she was sucking air into her scalded, much-abused lungs, he caught her off guard by scooping her into his arms.

She let out a startled yip to find herself suddenly horizontal, literally swept off her feet.

"What are you doing?"

"What do you think?" he retorted, not the least bit out of breath, even though she was still struggling not to pant.

Now that he wasn't muddling her mind with steamy kisses and subtle strokes of his hands up and down her sides, she could almost think straight, and she knew this wasn't right. Knew they couldn't do what he was carrying her off to do.

Pressing a palm to his rock-solid shoulder and wiggling slightly in his embrace, she said, "Eli, no. We can't do this."

"Yes," he told her in no uncertain terms. "We can."

Reaching the bedroom doorway, he elbowed open the pocket doors and headed straight for the massive king-size mattress at its center. The entire room was decorated in shades of the ocean—sand, turquoise, salmon—and the bed was made up with a thick golden comforter with enough pillows against the woven bamboo headboard to build a fort.

That's all she had time to notice, though, as he carried her to the side and set her on her feet so he could begin tossing those pillows onto the floor and tearing back the covers. Snowy white sheets in what she was sure was the finest Egyptian cotton lay beneath, just begging to be dirtied and rumpled.

Uh-oh. She took a step back in self-preservation.

Eli noticed her retreat immediately.

"Oh, no, you don't," he mumbled, grabbing her wrist and tugging her toward him.

Her hands went up to stop her from bumping into his chest, but he apparently wanted her to do just that, because he kept tugging until she made contact.

"We can't do this, Eli," she said again, trying to make him see sense.

"Yes," he returned with even more resolve than before, "we can."

He was all hard edges and single-minded determination, but when he looked at her, something in him softened. His eyes turned from coffee-black to melted milk-chocolate-brown and his lips parted ever so slightly. Offering her a small, cajoling smile, he brushed the side of his thumb back and forth across her cheek.

"Don't say no," he told her, barely above a whisper. "I know you want me. As much as I want you."

The words, spoken in such a heartfelt tone, made Kara's throat clog with emotion. Oh, how she wanted to believe them—wanted to believe him.

But she knew better. She knew this was just a momentary whim for him, a rebound fling to help him get over Laurel. And what better way to roll getting over and getting back at his ex-fiancée into one neat little package than by having a quick, tawdry, *meaningless* affair with her younger sister?

"What about Laurel? What about—"

He shushed her in that age-old fashion of placing a finger against her mouth. "She's not here, Kara. She never was. I've never brought her here, and she isn't a factor, not in this."

He continued to stare into her eyes, his hands moving to her hair and doing wicked things to her scalp. Things that made her want to moan. Things that turned her brain to mush.

Then he stopped trying to smooth-talk her. He stopped talking altogether. Tilting her head back, he slanted his mouth across hers.

She brought her arms up, linking them around his neck even as every other bone in her body turned to butter. It was useless. She was powerless against his charm, his blatant sexuality, against his very personality, every aspect of which she'd known and admired since childhood.

She might hate herself—and him—in the morning, but at the moment, she didn't care. Inside her head, she heard the immortal words of that famous albeit fictional Charlestonian, Rhett Butler: *Frankly, my dear, I don't give a damn.*

And she didn't. Not when Eli was kissing her like a starving man at his own personal oasis. Not when his arms were wrapped around her and her breasts were pressed to his chest. Not when the very thing she'd been wanting for half her life was finally within her grasp.

To hell with *should*s and *shouldn't*s, *maybe*s and *what-if*s. To hell with reputations, and propriety, and all the confessions and atonements she'd have to make once she got home.

Right here, right now, she was going to be selfish. Not just give in to Eli's successful persuasion, but do what *she* wanted. *Take* what she wanted.

And she wanted Eli. More than ever before. More than she'd thought possible, even after so many years of wishing, dreaming, fantasizing. Lusting from afar.

His hands were at her abdomen, fumbling with the miniscule buttons running down the front of her blouse. That small display of susceptibility on his part actually worked to make Kara feel more in control, more sure of herself.

Leaning back, she let him work. Not only because this was part of her fantasy, but she suspected it was also part of his.

His fantasy. A shiver raced down her spine at the realization that—at this moment, at least—Elijah James Houghton wanted her as much as she'd always wanted him. It tightened her throat, made it hard for her to breathe.

Then her blouse floated open and Eli's hands slid inside to cup her breasts, teasing the nipples through the lace of her bra with the pads of his thumbs, and she was not only breathing, but gasping with delight.

His mouth quickly followed the direction of his hands. Bending her back over one arm, he suckled the material, dampening both it and the skin beneath.

Kara could have sworn her head was spinning. Literally whirling around on her neck, taking the room with it.

From head to toe, she flushed with heat, her body slowly beginning to incinerate from the inside out. And they'd barely gotten started.

With his free hand, he found the tab of the zipper at the back of her skirt and dragged it down, the *snick-snick-snick* of the teeth echoing through the room like the boom of a cannon. He shifted just enough to let the garment fall past her hips to the floor.

Giving the back of her blouse a tug, he pulled it off her shoulders and down her arms until it followed the direction of the skirt, landing in a puddle at her feet. Without those two pieces of clothing, she was left in only her bra, panties and strappy sandals.

It was too late to turn back, and no matter how much she was wearing, Eli would have had her out of it in a blink.

Catching her off guard, he released her breast and pulled her upright, then in practically the same motion, scooped her up and tossed her to the center of the bed. She bounced there before using her elbows in an attempt to sit up.

"Ah, ah, ah." He gave her a dark look, pinning her in place with his expression alone. "Don't move. Not one muscle."

Still standing beside the bed, gazing down at her without ever breaking eye contact, he started to flick open the buttons of his starched white dress shirt. One at a time, methodically, with only one hand. The other was at his belt, slowly loosening the thin strip of leather.

"I might have to tie you to the headboard," he said, arching a brow as he tugged the tails of his shirt from the waist of his slacks. He shrugged out of what was probably a five-hundred-dollar suit jacket and the shirt beneath both at once, kicking off his shoes in the same motion.

"You've been so jumpy and so reluctant to be with me," he continued, slipping into a deep Southern drawl. "I don't want you hopping up and trying to escape at an inopportune moment."

The sight of his bare chest had her drooling. It was broad and sleek, with just a smattering of crisp, dark hair forming a T-shaped pattern across his pectorals and down to his abdomen. The muscles there rippled, attesting to the time he put in at the gym and calling to her like a half-off shoe sale at Saks.

Every inch of him was golden and lovely.

She licked her lips, watching as he lowered his fly and let the pants drop to the floor with a *whoosh*. Her heart stopped thudding in her chest, moving up to lodge firmly in her throat.

She tried to swallow, but failed the minute she glanced at him again—from head to toe and back up, getting stuck somewhere in between.

Looking at him, she had no problem with his threat to restrain her. The very thought of being tied down, at his mercy, made her go hot and turned her insides to molten lava. Never mind that the shape of the headboard didn't allow for anyone to tie so much as a shoestring to it; she would happily help him scout out other locations.

Even though she sounded like a pack-a-day smoker, she smacked her lips and swallowed until she could speak. "I'm not going anywhere," she told him in a graveled voice. "Not this time."

Nine

A jolt of lust tore through Eli at her words. He was pretty sure that if she'd tried to bolt, he'd have gone after her. Naked as a jaybird, if need be.

Never mind that his reputation as a hard-nosed business tycoon would be tarnished beyond redemption if his employees and the resort's affluent guests saw him racing across the shore after a half-naked woman. If it meant catching and keeping Kara Kincaid, it would be well worth the embarrassment and a short stint in the local mental ward.

But hearing her say she had no intention of running, no intention of changing her mind or trying to get away from him again relieved him of those worries. It also set his blood ablaze and made him want to get *her* naked as quickly as possible.

Climbing onto the bed, he advanced on her. She shimmied back a few short inches, but didn't get far before he caged her in with his body. His hands flat to the mattress on either side of her head, his knees against her thighs.

"Now you can't get away, even if you want to," he rumbled, staring down into those flashing green eyes.

"I don't want to," she said.

His entire body twitched. His skin began to tingle. And for the first time since adolescence, finishing almost before he'd gotten started was a very real possibility.

Careful not to touch her with any other part of his body, he dropped his mouth and kissed her. Slowly at first, savoring the taste and texture of her lips. Smooth and soft like rose petals or spun silk. Sweet and tangy like the strawberries they'd eaten earlier, with a hint of honey from the gloss she was fond of wearing. He nibbled, suckled, teased her as well as himself.

Beneath him, she writhed provocatively, making tiny mewling sounds deep in her throat. Sweat broke out along his brow and his pulse kicked up another thirty beats per minute.

Deepening the kiss, letting his tongue dance along the seam of her lips before pressing inside, he carefully lowered himself until he was stretched atop her entire length, pressing her into the downy mattress.

The lace of her bra scratched against his chest, but in a very good way. The feel of her matching panties cushioning his rigid arousal was even better. Rubbing slowly back and forth, he created a gentle friction between their bodies to match that of their tangled tongues.

Slipping a hand behind her back, he found the hook of her bra and released it, tugging the straps clear of her shoulders. But when he tried to remove the slinky material completely, Kara's hands came up, holding the cups in place.

As loath as he was to do so, Eli lightened the kiss, slowly pulling away until he could lift his head to look down at her.

"Don't," he whispered, holding her gaze. "Don't turn shy now. And don't hide from me. Ever."

She didn't say anything, but he felt her relax beneath him. Her hold on the bra went slack and she dropped her arms back to her sides.

He grinned—he couldn't seem to help himself. But not because she'd followed his orders. Because her acquiescence proved that she trusted him in one of the most intimate ways a woman could trust a man—with her body.

And because her breasts were magnificent.

Kara was far from fat, but she wasn't model-thin, either. She had curves—full thighs, lush hips and bountiful breasts—in all the right places. Curves that could make a man sit up and pant. Invited him to invent some first-rate fantasies or stick around awhile and explore to his heart's content.

Eli counted himself among the lucky few who were going to be allowed to linger. But he didn't have the patience or the fortitude to linger very long this time around.

Nevertheless, he relished the view. Her flushed skin, slightly parted lips, the rise and fall of her chest as she lay beneath him. She was at his mercy...but whether she realized it or not, he was also at hers.

He snagged her lips for a quick, hard kiss before trailing his mouth down her chin, her throat, the center of her chest. She arched her back, bringing her breasts even closer to exactly where he wanted them.

He caressed them with his fingers and thumbs, tweaking the nipples before lowering his mouth for his very first taste. She moaned, putting voice to the sensations swamping them both. He rolled one puckering bud beneath his tongue for several long seconds before moving to the other. He could have gone on forever, back and forth between those two soft, amazing mounds.

Could have, except for the fact that Kara raised her legs and wrapped them around his hips. Raised her arms and wrapped them around his neck. Her nails raked languidly up and down his spine; her thighs cradled him, rubbing maddeningly against his arousal.

Growling with mounting frustration, he abandoned her breasts and slithered down her body. She tightened her grip to keep him from moving, but she was no match against his size or determination.

She clung to him while he kissed his way down her torso, swirled his tongue around her navel, then dipped inside. Hooking his fingers into the waistband of her panties—which were little more than a scrap of white lace to begin with, held in place by an even smaller strip of elastic—he worked them down, slowly revealing the V of her femininity inch by tantalizing inch.

She squirmed against him, murmured his name in such a needy, breathless tone that he nearly gave in. But he knew what he wanted, and what she needed to push her as close to the edge as he was already.

Ridding her of the panties altogether, he tossed them somewhere off to the side, not particularly caring where they landed. Then he spread her legs, tucking them up and over his shoulders.

Kara gasped when she realized what he was about to do, but he wouldn't let her wiggle away. He pinned her in place, absorbing her heat, breathing in her essence.

Kissing her like this was just as pleasurable as kissing her mouth, but in a million other, very different ways. He used his lips and tongue and fingers to explore her folds until her mewls of protest turned to moans of delight.

She writhed beneath him, her hands tangling in his hair—whether to urge him on or still attempting to budge him, he wasn't sure. And it didn't matter. He had no intention of stopping until he'd wrung from her every ounce of pleasure she was capable of giving.

He could feel her body tensing, every muscle and tendon tightening like a bow as her nails dug into his scalp. Redoubling his efforts, he licked and stroked, driving her up and up until she cried out and went over.

He stayed with her until she calmed, floating back down to earth in a heap of boneless limbs she didn't even have the strength to keep wrapped around him any longer. The corners of his mouth twitched as he tried to hold back a self-satisfied grin.

Tried, but failed. He smiled his way back up the line of her body, trailing kisses all along the way. When he reached her mouth, he kissed her there, too, long and deep and hard.

Her hands, shaking with the aftershocks of her orgasm, came up to frame his face, caressing the slight stubble on his jaw. Eli groaned at the gentle touch, feeling his own skin ripple, the muscles beneath constricting in anticipation of what would come next.

Trailing his fingers over her hip and between her legs, he found her opening, slick with a mix of moisture from his mouth and her own feminine juices. Centering himself, he pushed inside. Slowly.

An inch.

He gave a silent but heartfelt moan.

Then another.

His nostrils flared as he tried to school his breathing. In, out. In, out.

And another.

Maybe if he concentrated on something else. He thought about his company. Of pending business, upcoming meetings and contracts that were sitting on his desk yet to be reviewed.

It didn't work. Heat and pressure built in his groin, radiating outward.

Drawing her legs up, he wrapped them around his waist. She crossed her ankles to hold them in place, arching up to meet him, which only worked to drive him deeper.

They gasped together, breaths mingling. And then he was fully embedded, buried to the hilt.

As taut as he was, every fiber of his being pulled tight with building tension and expectancy, he didn't rush toward the big finish. Instead, he held perfectly still, soaking up the sensations of being this closely linked to Kara.

He'd dated a lot of women. Been involved with them on varying levels, from meaningless one-night stands to lengthier, more significant relationships. Never before had he been anywhere near thinking the *L* word.

With Kara, though, it was easy. Just thinking about her made him go soft inside. Being with her, seeing her smile, hearing her voice and her smooth-as-Southern-Comfort laugh, warmed him from head to toe. And thinking about being with her *like this*…on top of her, under her, inside of her…made him go hard.

He'd certainly never reacted that way to Laurel. Not in the entire time they'd been engaged.

That had to mean something, didn't it?

Not that he was going to spend much longer contemplating the matter. He was busy with something more important.

Canting his hips, he began to rock gently back and forth, in and out. Kara's heels dug into his thighs and buttocks, and he returned the favor, clutching her bottom to bring her up on each of his downward thrusts.

They moved together like synchronized swimmers, every move in perfect harmony. But it was also *hot*. She cushioned him, squeezed him, struck a match somewhere deep inside that flickered, sparked, then burned him nearly to ashes.

Holding her tight, he rolled them across the wide bed, coming to a stop on his back so that she was on top. Once she caught her breath, she sat up, both hands flat on his chest as she straddled his hips.

She shook her head, sending her dark curls swirling around her face and shoulders. Her hair was rumpled and sexy as hell. Maybe because he'd been the one to muss it up.

Her cheeks were flushed, her lips rosy and swollen, and he'd done that, too.

A surge of possessiveness poured through him, making him feel strong and powerful. *Me Tarzan, you Jane* manly.

Reaching up, he tangled his fingers in her hair, mussing it even more as he tugged her down by those big, soft curls. He took her mouth in a hard, soul-stealing kiss, wanting to mark her as his own, ruin her for other men forever.

Lower, she started to move, shifting just enough to begin the exquisite friction of body against body, skin against skin, hard against soft. He released her mouth and she straightened again, curling back like Lady Godiva on her trusty steed. And in this instance, Eli had no problem whatsoever being her ride.

She placed her hands flat on his chest, the half-circles of her nails digging into his pecs. Her breasts hovered just inches from his face, pushed together by her arms. Those raspberry nipples, drawn tight and dimpled, called to him. He wanted to feel them, taste them, test their sensitivity.

He covered both breasts with his hands, weighing them, kneading them, using his thumbs to tweak their tips. Then he leaned up and took one rigid nipple into his mouth.

Kara moaned, sucking her bottom lip between her teeth. Eli grasped her hips, guiding her motions while he continued to play with her breasts as long as he could.

But eventually, instinct took over. Sensation swamped him. Bone-deep need drove him, and he knew it was driving her, too.

Falling back to the mattress, he sucked in gulps of air, a steel vise closing around his rib cage tighter and tighter while she gyrated on top of him. She looked like a goddess, but was doing things to him that only a temptress could manage.

His fingers dug into the flesh of her bottom as she rose and fell on him faster, harder, sharper. Her own breath came in pants, her eyes fluttered closed and he could feel her clenching around him.

She cried out, stiffening above him. Her whole body rippled with climax, sending shimmers through his own until he couldn't hold back and followed her blindly over the edge.

Ten

Kara was lying on her side, watching the sun slip beyond the horizon. It was a bright ball of orange, the sky glorious streaks of pink, yellow, purple, all sliding into the wide expanse of the gently rolling blue of the ocean.

Without a doubt, Eli had the best view of the entire resort. It paid to be the owner and CEO of such an amazing enterprise, she supposed.

It was one of the most beautiful sunsets she'd ever seen, and she'd never felt so happy, so comfortable, so satisfied and content. Or she would have, if guilt weren't swamping her in steady waves.

She'd just slept with her sister's fiancé. *Ex*-fiancé, but the *ex* part was so fresh and new, it might as well not even be there.

So instead of basking in the warm relaxation of afterglow, she was lying there worrying.

Worrying about Eli's arm circling her waist and what emotions or intentions it might symbolize.

Worrying about what she would say to Laurel when she got

home...or how she would ever again be able to look her sister in the eye if she *didn't* confess this weekend's sins.

Worrying about what to say to Eli, a man she'd known most of her life and yearned for almost every one of those years.

Being with him had brought to life a million fantasies, made a million of her dreams come true. But they couldn't last. And worse yet, she was afraid she might only be a temporary distraction for him. A rebound relationship designed to help him get over his breakup.

Which only added to her misery, because if there was one role she'd never played in her fantasies of being with Eli, it was a substitute for the woman he truly craved.

"This was a mistake," she murmured, still staring into the distance.

She should be leaping away from his touch, grabbing her clothes and fleeing his room, racing back to Charleston. Not that she had any idea what she'd do once she got there. Lock herself inside her own bedroom, maybe, and refuse to come out, refuse to speak to anyone until her guilt and humiliation wore off. If it ever did.

"No, it wasn't," Eli responded without missing a beat.

His nose nuzzled her hair, his lips grazing her earlobe. The arm around her waist tightened, pulling her even closer to his bare—and obviously masculine—length. He wasn't fully aroused, but he wasn't soft, and he made no secret of the fact.

"What are we going to tell Laurel?" she asked, her voice crackling with the sinking of her heart.

"Nothing. She has nothing to do with this. With us. We're consenting adults. We don't owe her, or anyone else, an explanation."

If only it were that simple.

"We didn't use protection." The flip-flop of her stomach at that knowledge—realized too late to do anything but panic—joined her rapidly descending heart until everything in her felt heavy and weighted down.

"I know," Eli admitted. "You got me so worked up, I completely forgot. I'm sorry."

He pressed a kiss to her temple, sliding his arm higher until it just brushed the undersides of her breasts. "I don't want you to worry, though. If anything happens, you know I'll do the right thing."

Wonderful. So if she wound up unexpectedly pregnant to her sister's ex-fiancé, he would "do the right thing" and marry her, giving even more grist to the overactive Charleston gossip mill. That had never been part of her fantasies, either.

She felt, as well as heard, Eli's long sigh. With a tug at her shoulder, he rolled her onto her back. She held the sheet to her chest, but otherwise just lay there, passive and pliant.

Propping himself up on one arm, he hovered over her, gazing down into her eyes.

"You need to stop worrying so much," he told her. "About other people, and about what they think. You're not responsible for the entire world, you know. Or even your family."

She raised a brow, knowing she should be offended, but lacking the energy to get worked up. "That's a terrible thing to say. I love my family."

"Of course, you do. *I* love your family. But you spend so much time taking care of everyone else that you never stop to consider what you need or want." He splayed his fingers and ran them through the hair at her temple. "You have a right to your own life, Kara. A right to be happy."

"I am happy," she protested.

"Happy enough," he agreed. "You're not sitting in a bathtub with a straight razor, that's for certain."

She wrinkled her nose at the image that created. She preferred to sit in a bathtub full of bubbles, with maybe some candles, rose petals, soft music, a glass of wine… And the only razor she took in with her was of the leg-shaving variety.

"But your first thought is always for others. What you can do for them, what they need, how you can help them. Even your job is about fulfilling everyone else's wants and needs over your own."

Okay, she was beginning to get some of her strength back. Annoyance was building.

"Since when is not being a selfish jerk such a crime?" she charged.

He shook his head. "It's not a crime. You are an amazing, caring, *selfless* human being. I just want you to admit that we're enjoying ourselves, and that there's *nothing* to be guilty about."

"When a person does something that hurts, or has the potential to hurt, another person, they *should* feel remorseful."

Eli cocked his head, still hanging over her, still stroking her hair. "Who are we hurting?"

She opened her mouth, a name popping immediately to her mind, but he covered her lips, stopping her before she could speak.

"Don't say Laurel." He sighed, a shadow passing over his coffee-brown eyes. "Dammit, Kara, you're not her keeper. She's the eldest sister, so if anything, she should be yours. But even that doesn't matter, because she is not a part of this. Laurel is a grown woman, she can take care of herself and make up her own mind, and that's exactly what she's done. She called off the wedding because she doesn't want to be married to me."

Licking his lips, he held her gaze. *Glared* down at her might be a better description. But despite the harsh lines of his face and the darkness of his glower, she could see the sincerity in his expression and had no choice but to believe him, no matter how strongly her gut told her to deny his words.

"And I'm fine with that. After giving it a bit of thought, I don't think I really wanted to be married to her, either. But I *do* want to be here with you now. And I want *you* to want to be here with me."

A sob worked its way up from her diaphragm and she swallowed hard to hold it back. She knew he meant what he said, *believed* he meant it.

She wasn't sure it was enough to override all of the issues

still clamoring between them, but for the moment, it was enough to make her forget.

Her hands came up to stroke his shoulders, his biceps, back up to cup his square jaw. "I do want to be here with you," she told him barely above a whisper.

It was easier to admit than she would have expected. Maybe because it was so very true.

A wide smile spread across his face, lifting the shadows.

"That's something, anyway," he murmured.

Then he kissed her, mashing his lips against hers, snaking his tongue inside to duel and suck and claim her as thoroughly as his body had during their lovemaking less than an hour before.

For long minutes, they were twined together. Her arms and legs tangled with his while he rested in the cradle of her thighs. His mouth devoured her, overwhelmed her, but in the best way possible.

When he lifted his head, his ragged breaths dusted her face with warmth. His smile was still there, making him look happy and youthful and carefree. The emotions were contagious, and she couldn't help but smile back.

"Now that we've got that out of the way, I have a proposition for you."

She raised a brow. "Another one?" Hadn't she been compromised enough for one day, one weekend, one lifetime?

The corner of his mouth hitched higher. "Yeah. Another one I guess."

She waited, her stomach taking only minor dips at the thought of what foolhardy endeavor he might suggest next, but it took him just a beat or two to fill in the blanks.

"Stay the week with me."

Kara's eyes widened in surprise, and Eli was glad he was currently lying on top of her, holding her in place. Otherwise she might have already exited stage left. As it was, she went statue-still beneath him, and he found himself holding his breath, waiting for her eventual, full-blown response.

The tip of her tongue darted out to wet her lips, and a stab of heat hit him center mass. They were in the middle of a conversation that needed to be finished, but there was no way she could miss his growing arousal. And if she was even a tenth of a percent willing to do something about it, he knew every coherent thought he possessed would be driven from his head in the blink of an eye, possibly never to be heard from again.

So he needed to hold his ground, grit his teeth and bear it until she answered him—preferably with the response he was looking for.

"I don't understand," she said. "I'm already staying with you through the weekend. More than I ever intended."

"I know, and I appreciate it," he responded, nudging her slightly beneath the sheets and waggling his eyebrows. Thankfully, she giggled, which let him know she wasn't on the verge of screaming bloody murder and hitting him over the head with the bedside lamp just to get away.

"I'm talking about staying the whole week, though. So you can do what you came here to do, and we can still have time to be together without a clock hanging over our heads."

"But what about Prestige? What about my family?"

He didn't gloat, even though he wanted to. The fact that she was questioning him, posing dilemmas he'd already mapped out solutions for, meant she was considering his invitation.

"You are Prestige," he pointed out, schooling his features and warning himself not to go too far too fast. "And the only event you're working on at the moment is unraveling my no-longer-upcoming wedding. No one would expect you to be in the office or pick up new events until after that would have taken place."

He purposely avoided mentioning Laurel—her name had been spoken too many times in this bed for his peace of mind, as it was. The fewer reminders of Kara's sister while he was trying to convince her to spend a decadent, illicit week with him, the better.

"As for your family…you know how I feel about that. We

don't owe them any explanations. But if you're set on sharing the most intimate details of your life and coming clean about something you shouldn't feel guilty over in the first place, well then, I would think you'd welcome an extra week's reprieve before that particular confrontation."

He shrugged, shifting so that his forearms aligned on either side of her upper body and his hands could frame the heart shape of her beautiful face.

"We're already here, in a spot a lot of people would say comes close to Paradise. We're obviously enjoying ourselves… or at the very least, I am," he teased, rubbing against her again in case she'd somehow forgotten that she had a heavily aroused man lying on top of her. "Let's stay here, continue to enjoy ourselves. Reality will intrude soon enough, believe me."

Rather than tense beneath him and try to push him away, or launching into a second round of arguments, her features softened, and he felt her release a sigh.

"Have you ever heard the term 'silver-tongued devil'?" she asked.

A question that didn't require an answer, but one side of his mouth hitched upward all the same. Her lips twitched in return.

"I think I've just met him," she confessed. "You're a very smooth talker, even for a Southerner."

"Only when I'm properly motivated," he told her, slipping into an even deeper Carolina drawl. "And you, darlin', are very proper motivation."

Lowering his head, he covered her mouth, going for a drawn-out kiss meant to persuade. The downside being that attempting to turn her soft and pliant had the exact opposite effect on him. He went hard and ready, and it was all he could do not to slide into her right that minute, bringing them both to an almost immediate climax.

But he'd been careless once, and owed her better than that next time around.

Pulling away—reluctantly—he leaned across her, careful not to crush her, and dipped into the top bureau drawer. He came out with the box of condoms he kept there just in case, though he'd never before had reason to use them.

"I promise to be more careful from now on, but we only have twelve of these, so I may have to run down to the gift shop and buy more."

"That's rather brash of you," she replied.

"We'll be together for a week. A case of condoms may not be enough."

She chuckled. "Now I know how you managed to build your very own hotel empire in only a matter of years—all that cocky self-confidence drove you."

"Of course. You don't think I got where I am on my good looks alone, do you?"

"Oh, and modest, too!"

Her humor and lightheartedness were contagious, and soon they were both laughing.

Had he ever laughed in bed before? With a woman and while he was sporting an impressive erection, that was, rather than simply sitting alone, catching up on paperwork and watching something funny on television.

If he had, he couldn't recall it. In his world, sex and hilarity didn't mix. But now that he was experiencing it firsthand, he found that he liked it. He could see himself laughing in bed with Kara again and again. Even doing things purposely to amuse her so that they could.

He would pour champagne into her belly button and noisily slurp it out…dot her nipples with whipped cream and chocolate sauce, and see how many tries it took to get the cherries to stick… With a bit of thought, he could probably even come up with a couple ideas that didn't involve food, too.

Of course, there was no time like the present, and he realized suddenly that he was famished—for more than just Kara, though she was definitely on the menu. But with the exception of a few nibbles of strawberry when they'd first arrived, neither of them had eaten since breakfast, so it was high time to remedy that.

Rolling away from her, he reached for the telephone and dialed room service.

Eli ordered appetizers, entrees and all of the ingredients for the hot fudge sundae he was suddenly craving—provided he could eat it off of Kara's ripe, voluptuous body. Then he asked them not to deliver it for another hour. That should give him enough time to ravish her at least once without any awkward interruptions.

"Expecting company?" Kara asked as he turned back around.

"No, why?"

"You ordered enough food to feed the U.S. Olympic team."

Shrugging that off, he said, "I'm hungry. But we have time before everything arrives to put at least one of these to good use." He shook the box of protection as he returned to her, gathering her into his arms.

She gave a long, exaggerated sigh. "Fine. But do me a favor—if you do have to go down to the gift shop for more of those, put on a disguise first. Bad enough everyone who works here knows I'm staying in your suite with you, I don't need them knowing we're having sex, too."

He quirked a brow. Surely she couldn't be that naive. "Hate to break it to you, sugar, but chances are they're already thinking that's exactly what we're up here doing."

Her mouth folded into a proper moue and she lowered her lashes in the best imitation of Scarlett O'Hara he'd ever seen.

"Presuming and knowing are two different things," she told him primly.

Eli started to chuckle, then bit back the sound, doubting she would appreciate him being amused by her modesty. He might think it unnecessary, but it was obviously important to her. And if it was important to her...

"All right. But you may have to help me go incognito. I left my Groucho Marx glasses in my other overnight bag."

"That's okay," she said, taking the box from him, opening it, and removing a single foil square. She waggled it in front of him between two slim fingers. "I'll lend you one of my sun-dresses and a pair of heels. No one will suspect a thing."

Snatching the foil packet away from her, he set it and the box of others aside. "I am *not* dressing up as a woman. Not even to protect your modesty," he told her in no uncertain terms.

She shrugged, feigning nonchalance when he could clearly tell she was biting back a grin.

"Suit yourself. You're the one who wants to extend our visit to a full week so we can stay in your suite and have hot, sweaty monkey sex. I was just trying to help."

For the count of twenty, he simply stared at her in astonish-ment. Where had *this* Kara come from? he wondered.

Slapping his arm out, he grabbed the loose condom and the box of extras right along with it, dragging the entire bunch back beside them.

"To hell with it," he growled, ripping the corner of the first packet open with his teeth. "I'll wear the dress."

Eleven

Kara never did make Eli wear one of her dresses—not that he would have fit into it, if he'd tried. But she wouldn't let him shop for fresh protection in his own resort's gift shop, either. Her face flamed at the very thought of the clerk knowing exactly who he was using those condoms with, and then running off to spread the news with every other employee.

At least this way she could still walk through the lobby with her head held high. Speak to the room-service waiters, registration receptionists and current event coordinator, Diane, with only a small spot of self-conscious color reddening her cheeks.

Then again, she'd compromised her family loyalties, her entire belief system and a good chunk of her self-respect to spend the week with him. It was the most clandestine, illicit and guilt-ridden affair she'd ever participated in or even heard about, so as far as she was concerned, he owed her one. Or twenty.

She owed him one, too, though. She'd come to Seabrook Island to investigate and revamp his event planning system... or at least that's the request he'd made in order to get her down here so he could sex her up, down and sideways, the lying bas-tard…and she intended to do that before they headed back to Charleston. If she didn't, she would forever know that she'd run off with her sister's ex-fiancé for a week of sex on the beach—or darn close to it—without even the guise of doing actual work.

Thankfully, Eli was of the same mind. Oh, he took advan-tage of every opportunity to sneak up behind her and kiss the sensitive spot beneath her ear…or pull her into his arms for a hot, demanding kiss…or tug at the knot of her towel just after she'd stepped from the shower, getting her dirty all over again (in the very best way) before she could dry off and dress.

But he'd also admitted that there was some business he could attend to as long as they were at the resort. Work that, if he took care of it during their current visit, would save him another trip at the end of the month.

So while he was off picking up protection for whatever erotic trouble he planned to start after they finished a private dinner…and taking care of *his* work, she'd decided to bite the bullet and sit down with Diane.

It wasn't that Kara was nervous, exactly, but from the moment she'd first met the woman, she'd gotten the feeling Diane Montgomery didn't care for her. Maybe because Eli was an eligible bachelor of the rich and handsome variety and she had her eye on him for herself. Kara could certainly understand the other woman's jealousy, if that was the case.

Of course, if Diane had confronted her about that at their first meeting, Kara would have laughed and shrugged it off. Her own secret, long-term feelings for Eli notwithstanding, she *hadn't* thought she was here to sleep with him. She probably would have handed him over on a silver platter, much as she had when she'd first noticed Eli and Laurel getting involved. Instead of jumping up and declaring her own longtime feelings for him, she'd kept her mouth shut and suffered in agonizing silence.

The other reason Diane might have for disliking Kara on sight was that she suspected Eli had brought her here to…

evaluate her work, dissect her past efforts and possibly even take over her position at the resort. Eli had never said as much, at least not within Kara's hearing, but that didn't mean word hadn't gotten around that that might be his purpose.

Which meant Kara had to be very careful about how she handled things. She needed to do right by Eli and figure out how well his on-site event planner was doing her job, but without making the woman feel as though she was undergoing an IRS audit. Something Kara should be able to handle quite easily...as long as Diane's discomfort around her was professional rather than personal.

As professional as Kara needed to be, she also had to keep things casual, otherwise Diane would be put off from the very start. To that end, she was wearing a simple sundress perfect for the cool spring weather, with flat, strappy sandals and no pantyhose. She'd also kept her jewelry to a minimum to avoid looking too flashy. Small, gold hoop earrings, a braided gold necklace and matching bracelet, and one filigree ring on the middle finger of her right hand.

Crossing the wide-open lobby, she made her way down a series of tiled hallways toward a rear section of the resort where the offices were kept. She found Diane's quickly, thanks to the clearly marked doors and Eli's detailed directions.

He'd offered to take her, actually, and sit in on her first meeting with Diane. To her mind, having him there could only make things worse. It would put Diane even more on edge, and make Kara feel self-conscious, as well. So she'd said thank-you, but turned him down, sending him off to do his own thing while she did hers.

Tapping gently on the office door, she waited for the other woman to respond before pasting a wide, friendly smile on her face and walking into the lioness's den.

For the second time that day, Eli caught himself whistling. Actually whistling. When he was far from a whistling kind of guy.

But apparently, being with Kara put him in a whistling kind of mood.

Talking her into coming down here with him had been inspired. Never mind that he'd had to bribe her with a work project and a possible future contract with his billion-dollar resort to do it...the point was, she'd come.

And just as he'd hoped, once they were settled in, he'd been able to lure her into bed with him. It hadn't taken long, either, a fact that caused him to preen a bit, sure, but that he was also just damn thankful for.

With only one short weekend—now extended to one short week—to convince her that *she* was the Kincaid sister he wanted to be with, he didn't have time for the usual amount of wining, dining and patient romantic wooing. Instead, he was taking more of a shock-and-awe approach.

If he could shake her up by getting her away from Charleston, distancing her from her business and family, then he might have a chance of getting through to her. If he could bring her here, sweep her off her feet, and show her a side of himself she'd never seen before, then she might believe him when he suggested they make things permanent.

He had to be careful, though, not to move too fast and spook her. Or smother her with his desire to keep her close, to be with her nearly twenty-four-seven.

How pathetic was that? He thought as he walked with purpose from his office on the first floor of the resort's main building across the lobby to the elevator. A thirty-five-year-old man who didn't want his lover of seventy-two hours out of his sight.

Some might call him whipped. And in a way, he supposed he was. Kara had certainly woven a mesmerizing spell around him in a very short amount of time, but it was a spell he'd walked into willingly.

Of course, it was no hardship to be in her company practically around the clock. In bed with her...in the shower with her...up against the bureau with her... But also sitting across the table from her, watching her eat and enjoying sparkling conversation.

She was witty and smart; opinionated, but not obnoxiously so. He could introduce almost any topic, and she would discuss it with him passionately and at length. Just the other night, they'd spent nearly an hour debating a handful of political issues, but rather than getting heated, he'd found her views astute and invigorating.

The elevator dinged as it reached his floor, and he stepped off, automatically scanning the suite for Kara. He didn't see her or hear movement from any of the rooms, but that didn't mean she wasn't here. In the bathroom or out on the balcony, maybe.

"Kara?" he called. No answer.

After checking the rest of the rooms and finding them empty, he moved to the bedroom and tossed the paper sack he was carrying on the bed. At Kara's urging, he'd spent the afternoon taking care of resort business. There wasn't much for him to do; he employed an excellent staff who handled most of the day-to-day running of the place for him. But he *was* the boss, and as the saying went, the buck stopped with him. Even if he hadn't devised a creative pretext to bring Kara to Ocean Breezes with him, he'd have made the trip down in the next few weeks, anyway, for one of his routine inspections and overviews.

It was good to have a lot of that finished and out of the way. Now he would be able to set aside business matters altogether and focus on what he was really interested in—seducing Kara. Again, and hopefully again.

He was still wearing the shorts and summer shirt he'd put on at Kara's urging to make his cloak-and-dagger excursion outside the resort property to the nearest gas station-slash-convenience store that carried condoms. He hadn't had to go far, thank goodness, and he was pretty sure no one had recognized him. Especially since he'd also been wearing sunglasses and a baseball cap.

Checking his watch, he picked up the nearest phone and called down to the kitchen to check on the progress of his earlier order. They were assuring him that everything would be ready at the appointed time when he heard the elevator bell ding again and the doors slide open.

That would be Kara. He'd given her a key card that would allow her entrance to the private suite of rooms whether he was with her or not. The only other people with pass cards were staff members, and none of them would come unless he requested it or gave them permission.

He met her in the sitting room, taking a moment to bask in her unmitigated beauty while her nose was still buried in an oversize book resting on top of a stack of other books and folders.

How was it possible for a woman to look mouthwateringly sexy and cute as a damn bug at the same time? The two descriptions were contradictory, to be sure, and yet they both suited her to a T. He was torn between wanting to grab her and tuck her against his chest in a tight, protective embrace…and drag her off to the bedroom to do some very adult, very nonprotective deeds with her.

Dragging her off to bed was close to winning out, but he'd made plans, dammit. It had taken him half the night to come up with the idea, and half the morning to put everything in motion.

By dropping the ball now, he would not only risk portions of his staff thinking he was losing his edge, but risk losing ground with Kara. That was more important than anything else, even satisfying his raging libido.

Tamping down on his desire, he cleared his throat to keep from startling her before stepping closer. Her head came up and she blinked like an owl. He'd been right about her not realizing he was there.

"That must be fascinating reading, to keep you so engrossed."

She made a noncommittal sound deep in her throat, then

closed the cover of the book and set the entire pile on the nearby credenza.

"What is all that?" he asked.

"Work. More than I expected," she murmured. Then she shook her head and met his gaze. "Sorry. I mean, scrapbooks, as well as paperwork for past events held here."

Eli cocked his head. "You've already formed an opinion of how things are running, though. I can tell."

Rather than respond, she started to nibble at her bottom lip, which was answer enough for him.

"Great," he mumbled, more to himself than to her. Rubbing a spot at the center of his forehead, he wished he'd waited to begin this conversation.

"All right, we'll talk about all of that. Later. For now, I have a surprise for you."

He'd been hoping for a spark of surprise, maybe the hint of a smile. Most women would be squealing and jumping up and down at his pronouncement, eager to find out exactly what the surprise was. But then, Kara was definitely not *most women,* a fact he'd known and appreciated from the beginning.

Instead, she looked wary.

He couldn't decide whether to be annoyed or amused by her reaction, but opted for amused. She was still a little gun-shy. Nervous about what they were doing, confused about her feelings for him and even more unsure about the ramifications of both.

So he would cut her some slack. Besides, if this evening went as well as he hoped, he would be one step closer to allaying all of her fears and convincing her that they could— *should*—be together in spite of the odd circumstances.

"Stop with the frown," he ordered with mock severity. "You're going to like this, I promise."

His assurances were met with continued silence and a doubtful expression. He just managed to hold back a sigh of frustration.

"Fine. I'll show you, then you'll believe me. Now, before we leave, do you need to use the restroom or change your clothes or anything?"

She raised a brow. "Where are we going?"

"I told you, it's a surprise. But we'll be a short distance from the resort, so I want to be sure you're comfortable and won't need to come back for any…emergencies before we're through."

She seemed to think about that for a moment, then gave a sharp nod. "Give me just a minute."

He did, watching her retreat into the bedroom. Several minutes later, she returned. Her hair had been brushed and tied back in a loose ponytail, and she was carrying a small clutch purse. Typical, he supposed, since she didn't know where they were going, and women rarely went anywhere without at least the bare minimum of a wallet, comb, lipstick, make-up case, the kitchen sink…

When she got close enough, he punched the elevator button, taking her hand while they waited. She didn't pull away, which he found encouraging. Hadn't, actually, any of the times he'd touched her or reached for her since the first time they'd made love. To him, that meant progress, and he would take what he could get.

Twelve

From the moment Eli took her past the reception desk to pick up a giant fabric tote with the resort's name and emblem stamped on the side, and then through the kitchen to collect an oversize picnic basket, Kara had a pretty good idea of what his surprise was going to be. She didn't let on that she knew, though, because she didn't want to ruin it for him.

She was also having trouble breathing, feeling almost overwhelmed by the emotions the situation evoked. He was being so sweet and thoughtful and romantic. And it had been a really long time since anyone—especially a man—had been any of those things to her.

Oh, she was sure Eli was on his best behavior this week. He'd set out to seduce her—a fact she still had trouble wrapping her mind around—and was apparently pulling out all the stops.

But since she was already sleeping with him, since he'd gotten exactly what he wanted from their impromptu trip to Seabrook Island, there was no reason for him to go above and beyond any longer. He could have just as easily ordered room service, then kept her upstairs, in bed, for the rest of the night. Something she wouldn't have minded in the least.

Instead, he led her out of the resort's main building through a side exit and down a narrow stone path toward the beach. Her fingers were clasped in his left hand, tangled up with the straps of the bag. In his right, he carried the woven wicker picnic basket that bounced against his thigh with every other step.

As they hit the sand, he stopped. "You might want to kick off your shoes," he told her, doing just that with his own.

She shed her sandals. Then, because his hands were already full, she leaned down and collected both pairs, letting them dangle from her fingertips. From there, she followed him instead of walking beside him.

Sand slid between her toes as her feet sank deep, slowing her steps. The wind blowing in off the ocean ruffled her hair, pulling thin strands out of the ponytail holder and whipping them around her face. The salty tang of the sea air stung her nostrils and lungs. Three sensations she absolutely loved.

Living in Charleston, she was very close to the water, but never seemed to find the time to truly enjoy it. She'd forgotten how refreshing the ocean breeze could be. How easily the sights and sounds and smells could bring almost instant serenity.

The farther they moved along the shore, the less "touristy" it became, giving over to rougher, rockier terrain. Then she began to notice the signs.

Private beach—no guests permitted beyond this point.

A few yards later: *No trespassing. Violators will be fined.*

And finally: *DANGER: Shark-infested waters. Enter at your own risk.* With a rudimentary drawing of a bloodthirsty shark devouring a hapless swimmer.

Granted, there could be sharks in pretty much any stretch of the Atlantic Ocean…or pretty much any large body of salt water, she supposed. It *was* their terrain, after all. But she'd never known the waters off Seabrook Island to be "infested" and didn't remember hearing any reports of recent attacks.

"Please tell me you haven't brought me here to feed me to the sharks," she said, raising her voice to be heard over the crash of the waves.

Eli glanced back over his shoulder and shot her a devilish grin. Pausing for a second, he waited for her to catch up so they could once again walk side by side, and she knew that if his arms hadn't already been full, he would have reached for her hand.

"Like that?" he asked. "I thought it was rather inspired myself."

With a chuckle, he added, "I asked one of my employees to section off part of the beach so we could be alone. He found that sign at the back of a storage closet, and we both agreed that if the others didn't deter visitors from poking around, the last certainly would."

"I should hope so."

A short distance past the last warning sign, they rounded a curve of beach and entered an area that was almost an island unto itself. Set back slightly from the rest of the shoreline, it was dotted with small trees and bits of grass, and a bed of sand that was flat and dry, with only a few feet at the front being hit by the surf.

Eli dropped the items he was carrying and began digging around in the bag. He removed a giant blanket and spread it out on the ground, taking extra time to straighten the corners. Then came plates and flatware, glasses and a bottle of wine.

"Sit," he said, waving a hand at the blanket while he moved to the picnic basket.

Setting their shoes aside, she folded her legs beneath her, careful to keep the skirt of her dress down around her legs. The steady breeze blowing in off the water wasn't helping.

As she watched, he laid out a platter of crab cakes pan-seared a golden brown, a bowl of chunky, savory southern slaw, and sautéed green beans with slices of onion and bits of crispy bacon stirred in. For dessert, there was a tray of tiny little berry tartlets topped with a dollop of what she was certain was fresh-made, not-from-a-tub, hand-whipped cream that he set aside just to tempt her. It was pretty much a GRITS's—Girl Raised in the South's—idea of a perfect meal, and the very sight of it had Kara's mouth watering.

Eli filled a plate and handed it to her before making one for himself. Then he opened the bottle of wine—a deep, dark claret—and poured them each a glass.

"This is delicious," she said after they spent a few minutes eating in silence.

"Our chef is one of the best," he said.

She cringed. "Actually, that's something I need to talk to you about."

"What—you're eating these amazing crab cakes that Jean-Philippe whipped up from scratch, and you have the nerve to imply he *isn't* one of the best chefs in all of South Carolina?"

He raised a brow as though he knew *that* was impossible.

"No, of course not. Jean-Philippe is clearly a genius," she assured him.

After all, she'd been the one to recommend him in the first place, back when Eli was just building and beginning to staff the resort. Eli had wanted the food at Ocean Breezes to be five-star…ten, if he could have managed it…and had asked for her opinion about hiring a head chef, since a big part of event planning revolved around catering.

"But I met with Diane today, and have been going over the files and scrapbooks for a lot of the past events that have been held at the resort."

"And…?" His voice was flat, unemotional. A businessman waiting to hear the bottom line before any decisions were made.

Feeling uncomfortable at having to point out the flaws in how his resort's events were run, and especially in the event coordinator herself, Kara's gaze skittered off to the side and she toyed with the fluted edges of her dessert tart. Finally, she took a deep breath, lifted her head and looked him in the eye.

"Diane has been offering guests primarily package deals. If someone comes to her wanting to hold their wedding here, she offers them standard, pre-arranged choices. Menus are already designed…the same bands and DJs are used over and over… decorations reused and stored between events."

She shrugged a shoulder and took a small sip of wine.

"There's nothing wrong with that at a certain level. I have sample menus for clients who don't know what they want. I have the names and numbers of several bands and DJs on hand, depending on a client's needs and the type of event I'm planning. And I have entirely too many decorations in storage myself that I pull out when necessary."

"But…" he prompted, ever a step ahead of her. It almost made her smile.

"But this is *Ocean Breezes*." She stressed the name, because in most of the high-class social circles Ocean Breezes catered to, the name really did say it all. It was one of those *Lifestyles of the Rich and Famous* destinations—the wealthy spent their weekends and vacations there, and the less-than-wealthy aspired to someday at least drive by and see how the other half lived.

"A luxury resort. A dream getaway for half of the United States. Anyone holding their wedding ceremony or fiftieth anniversary celebration here doesn't want the Surf and Turf Menu from Column B of the Seafarer Party Package. They want flowers and ribbons and other assorted frippery chosen just for them…a menu designed just for them…every detail to be exactly as they've imagined in their wildest fantasies, and unique only to them."

Leaning back, Kara blew out a breath, grateful to have that little speech out of the way. Now she just needed to wait and see how he would react.

"In other words," he murmured after several long, tense seconds had ticked by, "we're tantamount to the Plaza delivering motel-quality arrangements."

Her mouth twisted. "Something like that."

"What would you suggest we do to fix things?"

"I think that depends on how far you're willing to go."

He gave a low chuckle, turning the situation from awkward to once again comfortable and relaxed in a split second.

Reaching for his wine, he took a long, leisurely swallow. "I think you know me well enough to know I go all the way," he replied with a sexy wink, the double entendre in his words clear.

"I want my hotels to be the best, and Ocean Breezes is the crown jewel of Houghton Hotels and Resorts," he added plainly. "Whatever changes need to be made, whatever the cost, I want it done. So…what are your recommendations?"

Lowering her gaze to her plate, she continued to pick at her food while she told him the truth. "I think you need to find out what your clients want and give it to them. Don't just give them options to choose from, but be willing to fulfill their every desire."

"I kind of thought that's what we were doing," Eli mumbled. Then, "Give it to me straight, darlin'—does Diane have what it takes to do this job, or doesn't she?"

With a sigh, Kara dropped the fork she'd just used to stab a series of green beans and met his eyes. "I don't want to answer that. It's not my place to evaluate your employees. I mean, I know you brought me here to do just that, but…" She shook her head. "I'm a guest. I spoke with her for all of two hours. I haven't even finished going through all the files."

"But your instincts are already telling you something, aren't they? You've already made up your mind, even without proof." He gave an approving nod. "I follow my gut, too, when it comes to business, and I want to know what yours is telling you."

"Fine," she said, even though her chest felt tight and she really, *really* hated what she was about to do.

"Diane is a nice enough woman. She's probably very good with people."

"I've always thought so."

"But she doesn't seem to *care* about the events she's organizing. She seems to be…phoning it in, for lack of a better description. She likes the packages she's concocted because it makes her job easy. She never has to race around off-island searching for a supplier of pink calla lilies when they're out of season. Or spend two days on the phone trying to find a kettle drum band."

"And that's the sort of thing you do for your clients," he said, making it a statement, not a question.

She laughed, popping the beans into her mouth. "You have no idea. I once flew a magician in from Seattle for a birthday party and picked him up at the airport. On the drive, he made me hold three of his rabbits on my lap. They weren't in a carrier. And they *weren't* potty-trained."

"Oh, no."

His eyes danced with amusement and he was trying not to laugh, she could tell.

"Oh, yes. For the record, you don't try to launder a skirt that three rabbits have pooped and peed on. You throw it away, take a long, hot shower, and buy a new one the next day. Having the car detailed isn't a bad idea, either."

This time, he did laugh. A low rumble of sound that rolled up from his chest. "I hope you billed the client for all of that."

"I did," she assured him, silently remembering how relieved she'd been that the father of the birthday boy had very deep pockets and hadn't batted an eye at the exorbitant bill she'd handed him after the event. He'd simply written her a check and then sent several new clients her way in the months that followed.

"I can't envision Diane holding a rabbit on her lap, never mind letting it pee on her."

"And poop," she reminded him with a small shudder. "There was also poop."

He chuckled again, and she reached across the blanket to smack him on the arm.

"I'm sorry," he said, not sounding the least bit sorry, since he was still shaking with mirth. "But I've got a picture in my head now, and it's really funny."

"I'm sure it is. Did I mention that the magician was in costume the entire time? But not your typical magician's outfit. He was wearing a sparkly purple jumpsuit, complete with full-length cape. Imagine walking through the airport with someone dressed like *that*. Getting him through security on his way out of town was a nightmare."

He was imagining it, and rolling with laughter. He wasn't even trying to control himself, but was flat on the ground, holding his stomach and guffawing. And the terrible thing was that *she* was laughing right along with him.

"All right," she admitted after he'd settled down and she'd caught her own breath. "I suppose it was somewhat funny—*after* the fact. But my point, if you'd allow me to finish making it before you find any more amusement at my expense," she added with mock severity, "is that you have to be willing to go above and beyond to give your clients the best day, the most memorable event, of their lives. I don't think they're getting that from Ocean Breezes right now, and I think if they were, you'd get more bookings and word-of-mouth endorsements."

Back to serious business mode, Eli said, "I guess I'll have to let Diane go, then. Would you be willing to take over for her?"

Kara sat back slightly, eyes going wide. "You're offering me a job? *Her* job?"

"If you're interested."

"I— You— But—" Brushing her hands over her face, she took a minute to collect her thoughts, then tried again. "I'll be happy to help you out, you know that. But I can't give up Prestige and leave Charleston to come down here and work for you. I'm sorry."

"Of course not. I would never ask you to give up your business. You've worked too hard to get it off the ground and make it a success. I was thinking more along the lines of you splitting your time between Charleston and the island—at least to start. Then maybe hiring a few very capable employees to help you at Prestige so that one of them can come down here to work for the resort full-time."

She must have taken too long to respond, because he prompted her. "You have been wanting to hire extra staff for Prestige Events, haven't you? Someone to help you out so you don't have to run things single-handedly."

"I have," she said, with no little bit of awe leaking into her tone. "I just didn't know you knew that."

He flashed her a grin.

"I know more than you think. Of course, it helps that I'm wildly intelligent, pay close attention when I need to, and am invited to Sunday dinner with your family every week."

She smiled back. "There is that."

"This would be the perfect opportunity to finally do it. You would oversee everything, but one of your employees could be here five days a week—or even three, if that's all that's warranted—to run things to your standards."

It was tempting, very tempting. Gnawing her lower lip, she considered it from every angle. And then she realized that she couldn't possibly make a decision like that right here, right now. She needed more time to really think about it and reach a smart, informed conclusion.

"I'm not saying no," she told him after a moment, "but I can't say yes, either. Not yet. May I make a suggestion?"

He quirked a brow. "I thought that was the whole point of this conversation."

"Let Diane stay on. Let me work with her to plan a big summer to-do. A barbecue on the beach, maybe, or a lobster bake. Something substantial and seasonal and open to everyone. Use it to promote the resort, and show the world what kind of events can be held here, as well as the quality of care you offer when guests book special occasions with Ocean Breezes."

"All right, I like that idea. Then what?"

"We'll see if Diane rediscovers her enthusiasm for the job. It may simply be that she's gotten into a rut, and having something new and unique to work on will put her back on track. If not, you can consider terminating her, and I'll reconsider your offer to hire on extra help and station someone here on a semi-permanent basis. It will cost you, though," she warned him.

He grinned. "I'd expect nothing less. But you get what you pay for in life, and I'm willing to pay for the very best."

"You," she said, waggling a finger at him, "are trying to

butter me up with all this talk of taking over your event planning for the resort, hiring on employees for Prestige and having an unlimited expense account."

"I don't remember saying anything about an unlimited expense account."

"Oh," she said, glancing down at her nails as though examining her manicure and feigning innocence. "I could have sworn you did."

"Nice try," he tossed back, lips curled in a smile.

She lifted a shoulder. Chances were, if she did end up working for him on an extended basis, she wouldn't even need an expense account; he would readily pay whatever she charged without argument. That's just the kind of man he was. Especially since he knew how honest she was and that she would never cheat him out of so much as a dime.

"So what am I buttering you up for, do you think?"

"Sex."

That caught him off guard, and she had the pleasure of watching his face go slack at her forthrightness. She didn't imagine it was a feeling he experienced very often and nearly grinned that she'd managed to surprise him.

"You just want me for my body," she added, curious to see what his reaction would be to that slightly loaded observation.

"You're wrong about the 'just' part," he told her in a low voice, staring into the liquid depths of her emerald-green eyes, "but I definitely want your body."

"Sex on the beach?" she teased, running her fingers through his hair, along the curve of his scalp, down to his nape and up again. "I thought that was a mixed drink."

He waggled his brows, sliding his hand from her waist to the underside of her breast. "How do you think it got its name?"

At that, he began to nuzzle her neck, running his tongue in featherlight strokes along her soft skin. She let her head fall back and gave a low purr.

"I've never had sex on the beach," she murmured, her words

beginning to slur as desire thickened her blood. "The act or the drink."

With a chuckle against the silken flesh of her collarbone, he said, "We'll rectify that, I promise. Sex first, room service later."

"What if I want the room service now? I am feeling a bit parched."

Eli knew darn well she was teasing him, but he happened to be in a good mood. Having a beautiful, willing, soon-to-be-naked woman in his arms had a way of doing that to a man.

"If you're really thirsty," he said, as he continued to dot her body with kisses, "I'll call now. You'll have a drink in your hand in ten minutes. Only problem is, by the time the waiter gets here, you'll be naked and under me. Do you really want to risk that?"

She tensed a fraction, and he heard her swallow. "No," she responded primly, "I don't think I do. So sex first, drinks later."

He nodded. "Smart decision."

"I'm a smart woman."

"Yes, you are. A damn sexy one, too," he added, running his palm up her calf, the inside of her thigh, and past the hem of her skirt.

Her lips curved in a wide grin. "I'm glad you think so. I think you're pretty damn sexy yourself."

"Together, we made a damn sexy couple," he quipped. His fingers toyed with the elastic edging of one leg opening of her panties, threatening over and over again to delve beneath. "Who are about to have damn sexy sex on a very private beach."

"Mmmmm." She rolled the sound around in her mouth, letting her head fall back as his mouth trailed the valley between her breasts. "I'm becoming less and less interested in the drink by the minute."

"Good. Now let's see if I can get you more and more interested in the act."

Thirteen

Early the next morning, Kara was reconsidering her decision to turn down Eli's offer of a full-time position at Ocean Breezes. The resort was gorgeous. The island was gorgeous. The people were friendly and accommodating.

Could anything be better than waking up in the morning to the sound of the ocean lapping against the shore? Or the smell of the tangy salt air? Or the sight of the sun rising on the far side of the water, slowly turning it from onyx black to sapphire blue?

It was paradise, pure and simple. Heaven on earth.

Or maybe that was the happiness talking. As often as she'd cautioned herself not to get caught up in the romanticism of this weeklong getaway with the man of her dreams, it seemed she'd fallen and fallen hard.

A picnic on the beach. Gulls floating overhead. A gorgeous man sitting across from her. Delicious food, amazing surroundings, better company.

He'd flattered her, romanced her, listened to her, laughe

with her. And then he'd closed the distance between them and kissed her, caressed her, made love to her.

Right there on the beach, where anyone could have seen. Except no one did because he'd cordoned off the area ahead of time with warning signs and threats of shark attacks.

And he'd delivered on his promise of letting her try a Sex on the Beach—the cocktail this time—soon after they'd enjoyed the real thing.

How could any woman resist?

She certainly couldn't. And she was getting tired of trying.

After returning to their room from the picnic dinner and sandy-but-worth-it seduction, they'd both needed showers. She hadn't voiced a word of protest when he'd started the water running, stripped her of her clothes and then his own, and climbed in with her.

Less than a week ago, she would have screeched, slapped at his hands and fought him every step of the way. Not because she didn't want it, but because she didn't think she *should* want it. Or had the right to another woman's man—her sister's man.

Somewhere along the way, however, her guilt over her possible betrayal of her sister had started to fade away until all she was left with was want and need and love for Eli Houghton. She'd also started to believe that he might have true feelings for her. Not just a need for hot and dirty rebound sex, not just a desire for revenge against Laurel, but actual romantic and serious emotions for *her*. It warmed her, made her feel fuzzy and cozy like a comfortable old sweater.

She laughed to herself, glad no one else was around to hear her as she wandered through the hallways at the rear of the resort's main building. Comparing her newfound adoration for Eli to an old piece of clothing might not sound very poetic, but it was apt. There were some items in her closet that she absolutely loved and wore on days when she was feeling sad or nostalgic. She would never get rid of them, and if anything ever happened to them, she knew she would probably cry.

And just as she suddenly had an urge to go home and climb

into her favorite cable-knit sweater—which would have been perfect for the beach; she really should have brought it with her—she had a sudden urge to see Eli. See him, touch him, talk to him. Just to be close to him and ask how his day was going so far.

Never mind that they'd been together less than an hour ago. She'd awakened wrapped in his arms, pressed like cellophane to his hard, hot body exactly as they'd fallen asleep after a final, incredible bout of lovemaking that had nearly sent her eyeballs rolling back in her head.

And then they'd made love again. She'd never realized how much she enjoyed morning sex, but with Eli, she was practically a nymphomaniac. Morning, noon or night…bed, floor, sofa, sandy beach or the backseat of the car… Anywhere he wanted her, she was more than willing. And if he didn't approach her first, she was more than happy to initiate.

But as much as she might want to track him down and jump his bones, she wouldn't. She would maintain her composure, act like the lady her mother had raised her to be and wait until they were alone again, likely much later that night. *Sigh*.

She would fill the hours until then doing what she'd set out to do when they'd parted ways the first time—tour the resort buildings and grounds, and familiarize herself with both the layout and the leisure interests it had to offer. She knew most of the details already, but if she was going to be working at Ocean Breezes with Diane Montgomery to arrange a Fall event—she and Eli were contemplating August or September for the barbecue, a month when most people's summer vacations would be over, but the weather would still be nice and warm—then she wanted to be sure of her options.

So far, she was contemplating a number of activities for the event—tennis lessons, spa treatments, sailing and jet or water skiing, beach volleyball, possibly even horse-drawn carriage tours of the resort grounds and island. She just had to be sure that everything was both adult- and child-friendly.

Legal pad in hand, she headed for the same ballroom Eli

had shown her when they'd first arrived, trying to get a feel for the sizes of the different indoor areas at her disposal and then wanting to get a closer look at that gazebo again.

"Ms. Kincaid!"

With her hand on the door, ready to push it open, she turned at the sound of her name being called from down the hall.

"Diane," she said when she spotted the woman hurrying toward her. "I was going to drop by your office in a bit to discuss a late summer event Eli is interested in hosting."

"Sure, fine, whatever Eli wants," Diane replied with a distracted nod. "That's actually why I was looking for you—I want to talk to you about why you're here. I realize you might be feeling special right now, thinking Eli brought you here to take over my job."

Kara cringed inwardly. She'd been hoping to avoid just this sort of confrontation and thought she had by convincing Eli to give Diane a second chance. She opened her mouth to respond—though what she planned to say, she wasn't certain—but Diane barreled ahead.

"I can assure you, that isn't the case." The woman's nose went up a good three centimeters. "I'm here because Eli loves me. We've been involved for years. Why do you think he created my position in the first place? It's so that I would be here whenever he came down for a visit, without anyone knowing about our affair."

She shook her blond hair, surgically altered breasts popping forward as her shoulders went back. "It was important to keep our relationship a secret so that he could go ahead and romance your sister. I can't say I was happy about their engagement, but I certainly understood—Eli has always wanted to marry into a wealthy, influential Southern family to solidify his own growing fortune and reputation. Your sister was going to be a trophy wife. I'm the one Eli truly wants to be with."

"Excuse me?" Kara choked out, feeling as though she'd been hit over the head with a two-by-four. She heard the words, understood them in a Webster's Dictionary sort of way, yet couldn't seem to put them in order or make logical sense of them.

"I have to admit, I was relieved when your sister called off the wedding. It meant we could carry on as planned. But then you came along, and I guess he decided to move forward with marrying into the prestigious Kincaid family, after all."

Swallowing hard, Kara struggled to maintain her composure. No matter how much she might want to burst into tears or kick Diane in the shin with the toe of her pointy-pointy shoe, she wouldn't give this woman the satisfaction.

"Why are you telling me this?" she asked instead, hoping her face was as blank and emotionless as she was trying to make it.

Diane shrugged again. "I just want you to know that—no matter what Eli might have told you to get you down here—there's no way he'll ever actually get rid of me and put you in my place. Even if the two of you marry and he gets the high society bride he's always wanted, we'll still be involved. But don't worry…"

She fluttered her lashes and gave Kara a cold, calculating smile. "I'll continue to take excellent care of him, in bed and out."

With that, she turned on her heel and sauntered away. Kara watched her hips sway from side to side, her waist-length hair bob as her long legs in their four-inch heels ate up the carpeted hallway.

For long minutes, Kara stood frozen in place, feeling dazed, confused. It was almost as though she was having an out-of-body experience, her consciousness floating far above her form while she watched and heard everything like a third-party observer.

When her head began to spin, she realized she was holding her breath and made herself inhale. Exhale. Inhale. Exhale.

The sea air she'd so enjoyed earlier that morning now smelled stale and rancid, making her sick to her stomach, and despite the April temperatures that kept the entire island cool, she was fever-hot and starting to sweat.

Pushing away from the ballroom door, she forced her feet to move. Right, then left. One step, then another. She walked all the way back to Eli's rooms without looking at or seeing anyone, without even remembering how she got there.

The suite was empty when she got there, thank goodness. She honestly didn't think she could handle facing Eli right now.

She'd loved him and thought he might truly love her. She'd fallen for his charms, begun to believe all his honeyed words and romantic gestures.

But all the while, he'd been playing her. Just as she'd feared, he'd come to her only after Laurel had broken things off. If he couldn't tether himself to one Kincaid daughter by marriage, he'd take another; apparently, he wasn't particular.

Guilt and humiliation swamped her. She'd gone away with him, fallen into bed with him, betraying her family, and for what? To feel like a first-class fool.

Retrieving her suitcase, she began to pack, her movements stiff and methodical. Tears clouded her vision, but she refused to let them fall.

Eli might have used and lied to her, but she'd been the one idiot enough to let him. She couldn't fix it. She couldn't go back and undo anything she'd done this week, and she certainly couldn't un-feel any of the feelings she'd ever felt for him.

But she could stop them in their tracks.

She could stop being so gullible and easily swayed.

She could leave Seabrook Island and never look back, hoping that her family would forgive her for her sins and her stupidity—if she even had the courage to tell them what she'd done, how quickly she'd gone from being her sister's maid of honor to sleeping with her sister's ex-fiancé.

Pulling her luggage behind her, she traveled back downstairs, all the way to the car rental office. Half an hour later, she was speeding away from Ocean Breezes and home to Charleston, leaving the resort, the island, Eli and nothing but tainted memories behind her.

Fourteen

Such a small, inconsequential noise shouldn't have the ability to strike fear in a person's heart, but when the brass knocker sounded on Kara's front door, that's exactly what happened. In the middle of steeping a cup of hot tea, she jumped, sending the spoon clinking against the mug and water splashing everywhere. With a curse, she reached for a nearby hand towel to sop up the mess but didn't make a beeline for the door. Mostly because she didn't want to answer it. She didn't want to know who was on the other side.

It had been a week since she'd driven back to Charleston, angry and alone and well over the speed limit. She hadn't told anyone she was back in town, not even her family.

Never mind that she'd originally felt guilty about leaving for even one short weekend…and then a whole week…given everything going on with the investigation of her father's murder and her mother being suspected of the crime. When it came to running home with her heart broken and her tail tucked between her legs, she'd been too distracted and miserable to think of anything—or anybody—but herself.

She was wallowing and acting pathetic, and she knew it. She'd been chastising herself for days, annoyed that she'd let a man reduce her to such a state.

And she was just about to shake off her melancholy…really, she was.

But if it was Eli knocking, seeing him again was sure to set her back and cause her to remain housebound for another month, at least. She'd already avoided a dozen of his calls and refused to play back any of the messages he might have left.

The knocking persisted, but didn't turn to full-out pounding, which made her think maybe it wasn't Eli. And then she heard the faint sound of a woman's voice she thought might be her sister's.

Abandoning her tea and the towel on the kitchen island, she made her way less than enthusiastically toward the front of the house. Family was better than Eli at this point, but not by much. She honestly didn't know if she could face them after what she'd done…what had been done to her…and the secrets she was harboring.

At the door, she peeked through the peephole and nearly groaned, letting her head fall against the cool wooden panel. Of all the family members who might have dropped by when she was still feeling like algae at the bottom of an abandoned swimming pool, it had to be Laurel. It just *had* to be Laurel.

"Kara," she heard her sister call out from the other side of the door. "I know you're in there. Open up—*please*. We're really starting to get concerned about you."

Kara's heart squeezed and she sniffed back a wave of emotion. Family—her family, at any rate—was always there for her. Always worrying about her, watching out for her, ready to leap to her aid or defense, if necessary. The least she could do was let them know she was all right.

Taking a deep breath, she straightened her spine and unlocked the door, opening it to a wall of bright sunshine and one very agitated older sister.

"Thank God," Laurel huffed, pushing past her into the house. "I was about to call the police or ask one of your burly neighbors to break down the door."

"I don't have any burly neighbors," Kara murmured.

Laurel was dressed for work in a taupe suit with chocolate-brown edging and a brown clutch purse that matched her heels. Even as upset as she obviously was, she looked completely poised and pulled together.

A sharp contrast to Kara's current state of dress, that was for sure. She'd been in pajamas or ballet pants and tank tops since returning from Seabrook Island, and since it was early yet—hey, it wasn't quite noon—she was still wearing the cotton shorts and camisole she'd slept in the night before.

Laying her purse on the hallway credenza, Laurel sighed and asked, "Are you okay?"

It took some doing, but Kara managed to hold back a ragged sob, nodding silently instead.

"Eli has been calling. Everybody. He said something happened at the resort and he's worried about you." She paused, giving Kara a chance to fill in the blanks. When she didn't, Laurel said, "Do you want to talk about it?"

"I really don't," Kara told her, not surprised when her voice cracked slightly. Swallowing hard, she cleared her throat and added, "Not right now."

Another beat passed, and then, like the wonderful sister she was, Laurel let it drop. With a cheery smile Kara knew was solely for her benefit, her sister put her hands on her hips and cocked her head to one side.

"Okay," she said, "you can fill me in later. Right now, you need to go upstairs and get changed. We're going out to lunch."

"We are?"

"Yes, ma'am. You've been holed up in here long enough. I don't know what's going on, and you don't have to tell me until you're ready, but there have been some new developments with Daddy's case that I thought you might like to hear about."

Kara's shoulders went back and she suddenly stood a couple inches taller. "What developments?"

Laurel grinned. "If you want to find out, you'll have to stop moping, get dressed and come with me."

"I haven't been moping," Kara protested, sounding petulant, even to her own ears. "I've been working. Quietly and alone." Often in the dark. But she *had* gotten some work done since getting back, in between bouts of feeling sorry for herself.

Laurel raised a disbelieving brow, and Kara sighed in defeat.

"Fine. Give me twenty minutes," she told her, heading for the stairs. "There's a cup of hot tea in the kitchen. Help yourself, if you want it."

They ended up seated at one of the outdoor tables of a local bakery-slash-coffee shop within walking distance of Kara's house, rather than driving to a sit-down restaurant. Partly because Kara was too eager to hear the latest about the investigation, and partly because she'd been doing almost nothing *but* eating since her return from Seabrook Island.

While Laurel picked at a giant cranberry-orange-nut muffin, Kara kept her hands wrapped around the oversize ceramic cup of her low-fat cinnamon dolce latte that she hadn't yet bothered to taste. For the first time all week, she wasn't interested in food, only information

"All right, all right—stop with the torture Tell me what's going on."

Wiping her hands on her napkin, Laurel finished chewing and swallowed quickly.

"You know Cutter Reynolds, right?" she began.

"Of course." Cutter was an old friend of the family. Kara couldn't remember a time when she hadn't known him, and he'd been acquainted with her parents even longer.

Laurel leaned in conspiratorially, even though no other patrons were sitting close enough to overhear or even care what they were talking about. "He and Mama have been having an affair."

Kara's mouth fell open, and she jerked back in shock.

"Mmm-hmm. Apparently, it's been going on for a while."

"Oh, my stars."

"And garters. I *know*."

"I can't believe it," Kara said, still feeling as though she'd been run over by a giant paddlewheel boat.

Although she didn't know why she was so surprised. If she'd learned anything in the past few months, it was that not everything was as it seemed…and that her family—her parents, especially—were exceptionally adept at keeping secrets. Big ones.

Her father spending years living a double life and carrying on with a second family.

A half brother, and what amounted to a step-brother, she'd known nothing about.

And now her mother's extramarital affair with a man Kara had always thought of as an uncle of sorts.

"None of us could," Laurel said. "Although, considering how Daddy was carrying on for so long, I don't suppose we should hold it against her. It sounds like she really loves him, and she swears they never got involved until *after* she discovered Daddy had another family."

Kara nodded. She wasn't surprised. Her mother was a true Southern lady, in every sense of the word. She might have strayed, but not until after she learned her husband had been unfaithful. Otherwise, Elizabeth Kincaid would have gone down with the ship, remaining true through thick and thin.

"Mama told everybody she was taking Daddy dinner that night. Later, though, she had to admit that the real reason she was at Daddy's office the day he died—" a fact that had moved Elizabeth to the top of the police's list of suspects "—was to tell him she wanted a divorce so she could marry Cutter. But at the time Daddy was actually…you know…"

Laurel trailed off, caught up suddenly in the emotion and

remembrance of having a loved one murdered. Emotions and memories Kara shared. Regardless of their ages, they had lost their father—in a violent and gruesome manner—which made them all feel like small, frightened children inside.

As though it had been choreographed, they swallowed past the lumps in their throats.

"I know," Kara whispered, reaching out to take Laurel's hand. They squeezed each other's fingers.

"When it happened, Mama was with Cutter," Laurel told her in a low voice.

"So Cutter is Mama's alibi."

Laurel nodded enthusiastically. "And that's not all. Nikki Thomas—you know, the investigator we hired to find out whether Jack Sinclair is doing anything to undermine the company—heard from some of her police contacts that surveillance cameras from a parking lot near Daddy's office picked up Jack's Aston Martin. It was parked there when Daddy was shot."

Kara's eyes went wide. "I thought he had an alibi."

"He does...or did, anyway. Several of his employees swear he was at his office all evening the night Daddy was killed. But this...well, video doesn't lie. This definitely casts doubt on that and points *away* from Mama as the murderer."

"That's incredible." Kara released her sister's hand and slumped back in her chair. "I can't believe I leave town for a couple of days and the whole world goes topsy-turvy. But at least it went topsy-turvy in a good way for a change," she added.

"You were gone more than just a couple of days," Laurel pointed out, raising a curious brow. "And then you locked yourself inside the house for a week after you got back, refusing to answer the phone or talk to anyone."

Kara winced. It was true, and as they said, the truth hurt. "I know, I'm sorry. I just...needed to be alone for a while."

Laurel took another small bite of her muffin and washed

it down with a sip of espresso. "Are you ready to talk about it yet? Because I'm ready to listen."

Her sister's soft tone, filled with concern and support, brought tears to Kara's eyes. Blinking them back, she said, "Can I ask you a question?"

Laurel chuckled. "That is a question," she teased. "But of course you can. You can ask me anything, you know that."

Taking a deep breath, Kara steeled herself, then met her sister's warm, moss-green gaze, so much like her own.

"Are you still in love with Eli? I mean, I know you called off the wedding, but do you regret that decision? Do you still have feelings for him?"

Laurel studied her for long, tension-filled moments.

"I never loved him enough," her sister said finally. "That's why I called things off. I care about him, as a friend. Despite everything, I hope we'll still be close. That we can still laugh together at Sunday dinners and run into each other at functions without any awkward, uncomfortable moments. But no, the way you mean…I don't still love him."

Kara held her sister's gaze—and her breath—for several more seconds. Then she looked away, unsure whether to be relieved or more confused.

"You do, though, don't you?"

Kara's head snapped up at Laurel's soft question. Her sister was watching her much the way their mother used to when she knew one of them had done something wrong, but was giving them the chance to confess before she doled out a punishment for both the crime *and* the lie.

"It's all right, you know. If you have feelings for Eli, I'll give you my blessing. Happily. You don't have to worry that you'll be stepping on my recently engaged-to-be-wed-to-him toes."

Kara had been doing so well. So far, she'd managed to keep all of her breakdowns private, bursting into tears only when she was alone and sure no one else would see.

But her sister's words, so heartfelt and sincere, put another crack in the dam of her emotions. And apparently, all it needed was one more crack to crumble completely, flooding her with every drop of guilt, anger, sadness and fear she'd been working so hard to hold back.

With a ragged sob, she broke down, covering her face with her hands as tears streamed down her face.

"Oh, sweetie."

Laurel's chair scraped the ground as she stood up and dragged it to Kara's side. Wrapping her arms around Kara, she hugged her close, stroking her hair and whispering for her to hush.

"It's okay, sweetie. Whatever it is, it can't be that bad."

Of course, that just made Kara cry harder, because it *was* that bad. Kara was a terrible, horrible person, sneaking around behind her sister's back to have an affair with her sister's ex-fiancé.

Meanwhile, Laurel was practically a saint. Handling her broken engagement like a trouper, giving her *blessing* to her sister who'd lied and tried to steal her old beau out from under her.

And now Saint Laurel was comforting her, absolving her of guilt and trying to make her feel better. It was enough to make a low-down dirty snake like herself want to slither out onto a dry, hot highway and let traffic run over her until she was flat and dead. It was no less than she deserved.

After Kara had soaked the front of Laurel's beautiful suit jacket for about ten minutes, and given herself a nasty case of bloodshot eyes, swollen nose and raw throat, her sister patted her back one last time before grasping her shoulders and pushing her upright. Tucking loose strands of hair behind her ears and away from her face, Laurel wiped her cheeks with a napkin, then sat back and fixed her with a stern, determined glare.

"There. Now that you've gotten that out of your system, tell me everything."

So Kara did. She went all the way back to the beginning, admitting to the crush she'd had on Eli since girlhood.

To which Laurel said, "Oh, honey."

Kara expressed how hard it had been to watch the relationship between Laurel and Eli develop.

"Oh, honey."

That she'd pushed her own feelings aside, struggling to be truly happy for them and doing everything she could in her capacity as an event coordinator to give them the best wedding possible. But that after Laurel had called things off and Eli had come to her for help—both with his own business and the dissolution of the wedding plans—she'd let herself get swept up, carried away…let herself pretend and believe and almost… almost…

Fresh tears spilled down her cheeks, and Laurel pulled her close a second time.

"Oh, *honey,*" she murmured again, stroking her hair like a mother comforting a distressed child. "You poor thing. Why didn't you say something—*years ago?* I never would have started seeing Eli if I'd known you had feelings for him."

Kara shook her head, which was still buried in her sister's neck. "He never showed any interest in me, and I didn't want to ruin it for you, if you were in love with him."

Instead of giving her another encouraging *tsk* or comforting pat on the back, Laurel laughed. Startled, Kara sat up, holding her breath and blinking her wet lashes.

"You know I love you," Laurel said, "and I would never want to do or say anything to cause you pain, but sweetie…you've got to stop worrying about everyone else and worry about yourself for a change."

With a sigh, Laurel reached for another napkin and started dabbing at Kara's newly damp cheeks. "You are a wonderful sister. A dedicated daughter. Nobody could ever, *ever* accuse you of being selfish or not being there for your family when they needed you. But you don't have to be a martyr for us. You don't have to give up your own happiness for someone else's, or spend your life being miserable because you don't want to rock the boat."

"I'm not miserable," Kara said in a tiny, quiet voice that certainly sounded miserable. At least, she hadn't thought she was. She might not have been deliriously happy, twirling around on a mountaintop like Julie Andrews in *The Sound of Music,* but *miserable* was a bit of a stretch.

"You're sitting here, crying into your latte," Laurel pointed out. "Your hair is a mess, your makeup looks as though it was applied by Picasso and when I arrived at your house this morning, you were still in your pajamas. If I'm not mistaken, the same ones you'd been wearing for a couple of days."

Laurel raised a brow. "This, to me, does not scream personal contentment."

Oh, my god, it was true. She was a mess. She *was* miserable.

Hadn't Eli said nearly the same thing to her back on Seabrook Island? Not the miserable part, but the part about always putting others first, not spending enough time looking out for herself.

That made two people who knew her pretty darn well telling her the exact same thing.

So maybe she should listen.

"Does Eli feel the same about you?" Laurel asked.

Her eyes stung and her throat began to close at the mere mention of him, at the flood of memories from their time together. But she *wouldn't* start crying again. She needed to buck up and face this head-on, even if it meant reassessing her life and the way she dealt with others—especially her family.

Taking a deep breath, she was completely honest. "I don't know. He said he did, but then the things Diane said… What if they're true? What if he was only seducing me because he failed with you, and he really is after the Kincaid name and fortune?"

Laurel frowned, mouth turned down and brows forming a sharp V over her wrinkled nose. "I don't believe that, and neither do you. We've known Eli for years. He's one of the best men I've ever met," she said with conviction. "Not only is he a millionaire in his own right, he's noble and honorable. He doesn't need our money, and probably wouldn't take it if we offered it to him on a silver serving tray. He's proud of who he is and what he's accomplished."

She paused only long enough to pick up her cup and take a quick swallow of her now tepid espresso. "As for wanting to ride our coattails or marry into the Kincaid family to better himself…" She gave an unladylike snort. "If anything, I'd expect him to avoid the very possibility like the plague, knowing how vicious the rumor mill can be with that kind of fodder. The fact that he'd date either one of us is clearly a sign of the opposite—that he *doesn't* care about our name or social prominence, and is perfectly comfortable and confident with who he is."

Kara hoped she wasn't grasping at straws, but what Laurel was saying made sense to her. Parts of it, anyway.

"What about him jumping from you to me so quickly?" she wondered. Half-aloud, maybe, but really wanting—*needing*—an answer. "He couldn't have been ready to marry you, then suddenly develop feelings for me in the space of a single week. Could he?"

"No, I don't think he could," Laurel said, her features softening. "I think maybe you're the one he's been interested in all along—even if he didn't realize it. He was only marrying me because he thought it was time to settle down and start a family, and we'd always been close. Good friends who could maybe grow to be something more."

Reaching out, Laurel took her hand. "But, honey, we weren't sleeping together. That's one of the things that helped me realize we probably shouldn't be married. We'd kissed, of course, but even that was…bland. There was no spark between us, no need to be together or inability to keep our hands off each other. We were *just friends*, and I was afraid that's all we'd ever really be."

The air got trapped in Kara's lungs and she suddenly

couldn't breathe. No sex. No spark. Just friends. Three things that definitely couldn't be said about *her* time with Eli.

With them, there had been enough sparks to light up the entire North American sky on the Fourth of July. The sex had been spectacular. They'd done it round-the-clock…and tried to find time to squeeze in even more.

And the *just friends* part… They were friends, but didn't think they could ever again be defined as "just friends." Maybe they hadn't ever been; maybe there had always been more between them but lying dormant. Lurking beneath the surface, waiting to be let loose.

She lifted her head to find Laurel grinning at her. "The sex was good, huh?"

"Phenomenal," Kara admitted, barely able to hold back a starry-eyed sigh.

"I told you," Laurel said, looking entirely too smug and self-satisfied. "He's always been closer to you than the rest of us."

It was Kara's turn to frown. "What do you mean?"

"Kara," her sister said gently, "haven't you ever noticed how solicitous he is of you? At Sunday dinner, he always finds a way to sit next to you. Even while we were engaged, he somehow managed to finagle himself so that you were on his one side and I was on the other."

She hadn't noticed, though thinking back, she realized he *did* end up next to her during most of her family's gatherings.

"He calls you 'sugar' and 'darlin','" Laurel continued. "He never used endearments with me. I was always simply 'Laurel'."

That was true. He called her those things all the time, she just hadn't realized he didn't also use them with her sister or other women.

"And whenever we all get together, he seems to gravitate to you. Sitting on the arm of your chair…hanging out in the backyard while you help Mama with her flowers…offering you a hand while you're in the kitchen putting together a plate of cookies or making a pitcher of sweet tea."

True.

True.

True.

"He never did those things with you?" she asked.

"No," Laurel replied. "He was a gentleman, don't get me wrong. He pulled out chairs, brought me drinks, walked me to the door after we'd been out to dinner. But he didn't look at me the way he looks at you. His voice didn't go whiskey-soft when he spoke to me the way it does when he talks to you. And he never took me away for the weekend so he could ravish me within an inch of my life."

Kara flushed at her sister's pinpoint accuracy—and the knowing grin on her face.

"I don't know what the deal is with this Diane woman," Laurel volunteered, "but I'd be careful about taking her at her word too easily. Talk to Eli. Ask him flat-out whether or not he's having an affair with her behind your back." Her lips twisted in distaste. "While you're at it, ask if he was seeing her behind *my* back, just because I'm curious. If he was—and is—then he's just about the biggest jerk on the face of the earth, and I think we should hire a mercenary to take him into the jungle, stake him spread-eagle to the ground, and leave him as fresh meat for big cats and flesh-eating ants."

The image made Kara chuckle, even though she would never actually want to see Eli subjected to such an act. Then again, if he was a cheating, two-timing S.O.B., he deserved much worse.

"But, really, ask him," Laurel suggested again. "Give him a chance to defend himself—or come clean, if need be. I'd hate to see you miss out on something *phenomenal*—" she winked, tossing Kara's own descriptive term back in her face "—over little more than a misunderstanding...or a third-party trouble-maker up to no good."

Propping her elbow on the table, Kara blew out a breath and rested her chin in the cradle of her hand. "When did you get so dang smart?" she asked her sister, slightly annoyed that she suddenly felt like she deserved to sit in the corner with a dunce cap on her head.

Laurel chuckled, reaching for the final bite of her muffin and popping it into her mouth. "I've always been this smart. You just never noticed before because you didn't want to admit your older sister might actually be able to teach you something about life."

They both knew that wasn't entirely true, but if Laurel wanted to gloat, Kara was more than happy to let her. This time, at least.

"Well, you've taught me something today," Kara told her. "Thank you."

"You're welcome. Though I'd appreciate it more if you were thanking me for keeping you from making the biggest mistake of your life…and for helping you find true love."

With a wide smile—the first she'd let slip out since she'd returned from Ocean Breezes—Kara leaned over and hugged her sister tight.

"Give me a little more time," she said just above her sister's ear. "Maybe I still will."

Fifteen

Once Laurel was certain Kara had no intention of climbing back into her pajamas and under the covers with a pint of fudge ripple to wallow in self-pity for another week, she agreed to leave her to her own devices. Seeing her home, she gave her a hug and a peck on each cheek, then headed back to work.

Her sister had nothing to worry about, though. Kara felt excited, energized, hopeful.

As soon as she shut the front door behind her sister, Kara tossed her purse at the hall credenza and raced upstairs, kicking off her shoes and beginning to undress along the way. To go out with her sister, she'd thrown on a simple pair of white shorts and turquoise camisole top embellished with sequins and beading along the neckline. But that wasn't remarkable enough for what she planned to do next.

Because her makeup was, indeed, a mess from her crying jag, she washed her face a second time, then left her skin to dry a bit while she rooted through her closet for just the right dress...just the right shoes. She didn't want to overdo it, though.

Look good? Yes.

Show Eli what he'd be missing if he gave the wrong answers or turned out to be a jerk of the first order, after all? Yes.

Look as though she belonged down by the docks, selling her wares to every sailor and fisherman who stumbled off a boat at the end of the night? No.

Look desperate or needy or gullible? Definitely not.

So she bypassed the "evening wear" and "beauty pageant" sections of her wardrobe. The "summer casual" and "work formal" collections were out, too. That left her everyday, nine-to-five clothes—which were actually very nice—and things she wore to luncheons or the country club.

Perfect.

She opted for a satiny slip dress in butter yellow with blue piping at the arms and throat, and tall blue bachelor's buttons at the bottom as though they were growing up from the hem. Next came a pair of retro wedge sling-back espadrilles, and then she was off to the bathroom to fix her hair and re-apply her makeup.

Half an hour later, she retrieved her purse from the floor beside the credenza and darted out the door. It took what felt like forever to get through midday traffic to the business district where Eli's office was located and make it up to his floor. She was positively vibrating the entire elevator ride.

With a quick finger-wave to the main receptionist, she headed down the hall to Eli's office. She'd been here so many times, she didn't bother to stop out front anymore, but went straight to Penelope, Eli's personal assistant.

The older woman was sitting behind her desk, fingers flying across the keyboard as she worked. She must have seen Kara in her peripheral vision, though, because her head came up the second Kara stepped through the doorway.

"Well, hey there, Miz Kincaid. How are you today?"

"Fine, Penelope, thank you. How are you?"

"Just dandy, thanks."

"Is Eli here?" Kara asked. "I really need to speak with him."

"I'm so sorry, hon, but he's not in. He took the whole day off, actually."

"Oh." Kara's face fell, taking her heart with it. She hadn't expected that and didn't have a back-up plan.

Penelope cocked her head to the side, giving Kara a sympathetic glance. "I'm not supposed to do this, but I don't think he'd mind me telling you. He's at the park."

"The park?" Kara asked in surprise. That didn't sound like Eli. Except for their time on Seabrook Island, he tended to be a bit of a workaholic. He'd rather be closed up in his office poring over paperwork than out taking a leisurely stroll.

"Yeah. Wannamaker Park. He'll be there for a few hours, at least."

"Thank you," Kara said, spinning on her heel and rushing out of the office.

"Good luck!" Penelope called after her.

Kara couldn't imagine what Eli was doing at the park. On a beautiful spring day like today, the place was packed. Children everywhere—running, playing, laughing. Parents watching, chasing, wiping runny noses and blowing on scraped knees. It didn't seem even remotely Eli's style.

Still, she was here, and Eli supposedly was, so she wasn't leaving until she'd either found him or scoured every inch of the park to be certain he wasn't here. Which was easier said than done.

She checked the playground and the picnic areas. Dodged skateboarders and bike riders.

Just when she was about to give up, she heard loud singing, and turned to see a crowd dotted by balloons and party hats. The group was mostly children, but children of varying ages with a few adults thrown in.

Moving closer, she found herself humming along with the off-key rendition of "Happy Birthday" as she glanced over everyone's heads, thinking perhaps Eli was standing on the other side of the birthday gathering, watching the festivities.

The song drew to a close, followed by a group outcry for

the birthday boy or girl to "Blow out the candles! Blow out the candles!" But when it came to that, six or eight of the children gathered most closely around the table leaned in to do the deed.

Odd, Kara thought, but though she was distracted by her search for Eli, Kara couldn't help smiling at the sheer joy emanating from the partygoers. Warm memories of her own childhood birthday parties, and those of her brothers' and sisters', played through her head.

And then, at the very center of the crowd, a man who must have been crouched down beside the picnic table stood. He was holding a large plastic knife in anticipation of cutting the cake, wearing a yellow, pointy-tipped, glitter-covered paperboard hat and smiling the widest smile she'd ever seen.

Eli laughed at something a young black boy said, and began doling out evenly sliced squares of the giant sheet cake to the two or three dozen other children dancing around, awaiting their sugar high.

Rooted to the spot, Kara watched him. He was dressed very casually in jeans and a blue chambray shirt, sleeves rolled up to reveal his muscled forearms, and looked more handsome than she could ever remember seeing him. Then again, they'd been apart for a whole week, so maybe she was simply starved for the sight of him.

She couldn't quite make sense of what Eli was doing in the middle of a child's birthday bash, but she didn't care. Her head buzzed and her pulse raced while she waited none too patiently for him to finish passing out cake. A woman beside him was adding scoops of ice cream to each plate, which slowed down the process and added to Kara's growing anticipation.

Finally, all the kids and most of the adults had their servings and were digging in, and she couldn't stand it a moment longer.

"Eli," she called out, hoping he would hear her over the voices of the boisterous children. "Eli!"

He turned, his eyes going wide when he spotted her at the edge of the party-hatted crowd. Passing the knife to the woman in charge of ice cream, he started toward her, weaving between children until they stood only inches apart.

"Kara."

He breathed her name, making it sound like a wish, a prayer, an endearment, and her knees went weak. Her heart pounded so hard, she was sure he could see it through her dress.

"I called," he said, shoving his hands into the front pockets of his jeans.

"I know. I'm sorry, I just…"

She trailed off. Now that she was here with him, close enough to reach out and touch him—which she wanted to do so badly her palms were tingling—she didn't know where to start.

"I was upset," she told him honestly. "I needed time."

Eli rocked back on his heels, fighting the urge to drag her against his chest and kiss her senseless. His gaze raked over her again and again, taking in the glorious fall of her auburn hair, her sparkling green eyes, those rose petal lips, and her womanly curves beneath a dress that was pretty enough…but would look even better in a pile on the floor beside his bed.

He couldn't ravish her just yet. They had some things to discuss first. Important things.

She licked her lips, and her gaze skittered over his shoulder. "What is this?" she asked.

He didn't bother looking. The noise level alone told him all was well and everybody was having a good time.

"Never mind that." He shrugged off the question, more interested in getting an answer to his own.

"Why did you leave the island, Kara? I thought we were fine."

Better than fine, actually. He'd thought they were well on their way to damn near perfect. Realizing they weren't, remembering the moment of panic he'd felt when he'd realized she wasn't just late getting back to the suite, but gone— and not coming back—caused his mouth to turn down.

"Then you disappeared without a word."

He watched her chest hitch as she inhaled deeply.

"Because I was hurt. And angry. And felt like a fool."

His brows knit. "Why?" he asked, even though he already knew the answer. He knew more, in fact, than she did at this point, but wanted to hear the situation from her perspective.

Rather than answering his question, she asked one of her own. Tipping her head to the side, she said, "Are you sleeping with Diane Montgomery? And don't you lie to me, Elijah James Houghton," she added in a tone that reminded him entirely too much of his mother, complete with a finger waggled under his nose.

He bit back a grin at her flushed cheeks and riled disposition. If she suspected he found this conversation entertaining in any way, he would be knee-deep in swamp water. She'd likely kick him in the shin or smack him with her purse in front of the entire park full of people. But it was almost impossible not to be amused and even energized by her barely suppressed outrage.

What wasn't amusing was the fact that she'd run away from him in the first place instead of coming to him with her suspicions and concerns…even her fury. If she'd stuck around to confront him while they were still at Ocean Breezes, they could have hashed this all out in a matter of hours and spent the rest of the week enjoying themselves. And each other.

But they were here now, and though he'd have picked a different venue for this discussion, he wasn't going to pass up the opportunity to work this out once and for all.

"No. I am not sleeping with Diane," he told her in no uncertain terms. "We were involved once, a few years ago, but not now."

Kara worried the inside of her bottom lip. "That's why I left," she said softly. "Diane told me you were having an affair. She said you had some sordid plan to marry a Kincaid just to get into the family and increase both your bank account and your social standing, but were going to continue seeing her behind Laurel's—and then my—back. Using Ocean Breezes as your own personal love nest," she added with a disgusted twist of her lips.

Eli scowled. "And you believed her."

She had the decency to flush. "Yes. Or maybe I was just afraid *not* to believe her."

Her gaze dropped to her feet, where she was dragging the toe of one shoe back and forth along the grass. Then her shoulders drooped and she gave a loud sigh before heading away from the party toward an empty picnic table. He followed, knowing they weren't finished with their discussion.

She perched on the end of one of the bench seats, setting her purse on the table and straightening the skirt of her dress to keep from flashing too much leg. He liked her legs; he wouldn't have minded seeing her flash a bit more of them.

Taking a deep breath and finding courage, she turned to face him again. "I let myself get comfortable with you, feel... maybe too much for you."

A stab of optimism shot through him. Her eyes were the dark green of summer moss, brimming with emotion as she spoke. He wanted to haul her into his arms right then, or at least reach across the table and take her hand, but he needed to hear this. He needed to know what she was thinking and how she felt about him now...before he told her the way it was going to be.

"I was really enjoying our time at the resort, but in the back of my mind, I don't think I ever truly believed any of it—anything between us—was real."

His scowl deepened, and he had to bite his tongue to keep from snapping right then and there. But if he stopped her now, he knew he'd never get the rest out of her, and he needed to hear it.

Holding his gaze, she said, "I couldn't believe you wanted me or cared for me as more than a friend, because you'd never shown the least bit of interest in me that way before. And it was *too easy* to believe that you were on the rebound from your breakup with Laurel. Not just a breakup, but practically being left at the altar. It wasn't much of a stretch to think you might be using me to get back at her."

Eli clenched his jaw so forcefully, he could hear his molars grinding to dust. "You'd better get to the point damn quick," he bit out, "because I've got something to say and I'm running low on patience."

Her lashes fluttered at that. She looked just about ready to bolt...which would be a huge mistake on her part. Birthday party or not, park full of witnesses or not, if she made one move to get away from him, he was going to tackle her to the ground like the Carolina Panthers offensive line and ruin that cute little dress of hers.

She swallowed, her chest rising and falling with her shallow breaths. And then, in a tone so soft he could barely hear it over the revelry at his back, she said, "I've been in love with you forever, Eli. Since the first time we met...all through high school, college, our adult lives... It broke my heart when you started dating Laurel. When the two of you started talking about marriage and asked me to plan the wedding."

Her voice cracked and her eyes glistened with moisture. Any anger or frustration he'd been feeling only seconds before washed away, replaced by keen remorse and the sudden understanding that he was a jackass. A complete and utter fool.

Giving in to temptation, he took her hand, linking their arms across the top of the plastic picnic table.

"Kara," he whispered softly.

She shook her head, blinking to keep the tears at bay. "So you can see why I didn't think I could trust your sudden profession that you had feelings for me. Or trust myself to trust you, for fear it was just my long-buried crush spinning out of control."

"Kara," he said again.

She licked her lips before they curved into a crooked, slightly insecure smile. "But I had coffee with Laurel this morning," she told him. "And she had this really smart idea.

She suggested I simply *ask you* about what Diane said, and give you a chance to respond. So here I am. Asking."

Her shoulders went back as she straightened her spine, her chest rising as she inhaled confidence along with fresh oxygen. "Are you in love with Diane?"

Eli sat up straighter, too. If they were going to do this, then they were going to do it head-on. No beating around the bush. It was no-holds-barred, all-on-the-line, do-or-die truth-telling time.

He met her gaze, looked directly into her soul, and invited her to look into his.

"No," he answered firmly.

"Are you sleeping with her—now?"

"Absolutely not."

"Are you still in love with Laurel?"

"I don't think I was ever in love with Laurel," he responded honestly.

"Do you still have feelings for her at all? Other than friendship."

"No."

Kara paused, her toe tapping wildly beneath the table while nerves coursed through her bloodstream. She knew what she wanted to ask next, but once she did, that was it. Game over. His answer would determine the entire future of their relationship—good, bad or indifferent.

But she had to know.

"Are you in love with me?"

Sixteen

Kara's heart lurched against her rib cage over and over again like a Mexican jumping bean while their gazes remained linked. Eli's eyes, dark and glittering with intensity, made her want to squirm, but she refused to look away until she had an answer.

The heavy, razor-sharp silence was killing her. Fear that he might say no or, worse yet, that his face would fill with pity at her awkward confession and pathetic desire for him, turned her insides cold.

But she held her ground, waited, and told herself that if he was going to break her heart into a million pieces, then it was better to be done with it here and now.

She could go home and lick her wounds later. Lord knew she still had the ratty pajamas, unmade bed and freezer full of ice cream ready.

To her surprise, Eli pushed to his feet, coming to her side of the picnic table and pulling her up to stand in front of him. Framing her face in both of his big, strong hands, he smiled, sending a shiver of warmth through her system.

"Yes," he said, his voice rough and graveled and sincere. "Yes, I'm in love with you. I think I have been for years, too. I just didn't realize it until recently."

Running the pad of his thumb back and forth across her bottom lip, he said, "I fired Diane."

He gave a small chuckle when Kara's eyes went wide as saucers.

"When I couldn't find you that last day you were at the resort, I went searching and ran into her instead. She admitted what she'd told you—sounded proud of it, no less. I think she actually believed what she said to you. In her mind, she thought we had a real relationship, while I considered our time together nothing more than a one-, maybe two-night stand. I never would have hired her if I'd known she had an agenda."

"So you fired her?" Kara didn't know whether to be shocked or flattered.

"On the spot. Ordered Security to stay with her while she gathered her belongings and see her off the resort property so there would be absolutely no mistakes and no confusion about my feelings—or lack thereof. I called you right after. And called, and called, but you didn't answer."

"I'm sorry, I—"

He covered her mouth with his finger. "I would have been back in Charleston that very night, on your doorstep with candy and flowers and my heart on my sleeve, but as luck would have it…disaster struck."

His mouth twisted with irony. "I don't know if she did it in an act of payback for bringing you in, or if she was just a lousy event planner, but Diane booked two large golfing events for the exact same time. Guests started flooding in, we didn't have enough rooms for all of them, the courses were double-booked… It was a nightmare. One I couldn't leave the staff to handle alone, so I stuck around to help get everything ironed out."

She nodded. She understood completely. And he'd said

he loved her, which pretty much made everything else in her life—everything else in the world—a non-issue.

"I only got back into town last night. Called you again," he added, "but you still wouldn't answer."

She winced with guilt, nose wrinkling, and he chuckled.

"I was going to come over, but wanted the timing to be right, and I was tired, cranky… I thought it would be better to let us both get a good night's sleep. Then this morning when I got to the office, Penelope reminded me about the party, and I had to be here."

He cast a quick glance over his shoulder, where kids with frosting smeared all around their mouths, and on their hands and clothes, had started chasing each other, playing hide-and-seek and breaking out the party favors.

"I was in charge of picking up the cake."

Something thick and warm unfurled at the base of her stomach at his admission. He sounded so proud.

"What is this?" she asked, just as she had earlier. Maybe this time, he would answer her.

"April's birthday party." At her questioning expression, he explained. "You know I was a foster child, and I lived in a group home as often as a foster one, until Mom and Dad took me in. Well, special occasions and reasons to celebrate are hard to come by in group homes—as are the funds to party properly."

She shook her head. "I didn't realize."

"Most people don't, but I've never forgotten how it feels to lie in bed at night and know no one remembered your birthday—if they even knew it to begin with. So when I started making good money, I made a point of going back. I visit every few weeks, arrange outings to museums or the zoo, and I throw big bashes like this for any of the kids who have a birthday that month."

Kara's chest tightened and tears stung the backs of her eyes. And this time, it had nothing to do with fear that her feelings for Eli might not be reciprocated. Instead, it had everything to

do with feeling like a worthless, self-centered human being...
and realizing that the man before her was not only wonderful,
thoughtful and self*less,* but that she'd gotten very close to letting him slip through her fingers.

Clearing her throat, she said, "You did all this?"

Color bloomed on his cheekbones. "Well, I had some help.
Penelope orders the cakes and decorations, reserves the locations, if necessary. But she lets me take the credit."

"I'm glad." Kara smiled, sparing another glance for the
young partygoers before returning her attention to Eli.

"Will you let me be involved next time?" she asked. "I'd
love to bring some presents or help come up with new ideas
for party themes."

Eli beamed at her, his grin wider and brighter than she'd
ever seen it. He gave her elbows a squeeze and leaned in to
press a quick kiss to her lips. "They would love that. *I* would
love it. We supply gifts, but they're more of the boy/girl variety, not child-specific. If you could help us personalize things
a bit, that would be great."

"Consider it done," she told him. And she meant it. His
kindness and compassion were contagious, and she could tell
these kids were a cause near and dear to his heart. Which meant
that—if things between them played out the way she hoped
they would—they were about to become important to her, as
well.

His hands brushed up her arms, stopping at her shoulders
while he continued to study her. Finally, he said, "I need you
to know something. I was never in love with your sister."

His voice was low and genuine, and an invisible weight she
hadn't known was pushing down on her, lifted.

"I decided I was ready to settle down and start a family, and
I thought we would make a good match. Laurel is classy and
sophisticated, she comes from a good family..." He shot her a
lopsided grin. "All the things you are, of course, but there was
no spark there. Nothing that kept me up at night or made me
crazy with wanting. *You* make me crazy with wanting, Kara.

And you definitely keep me up at night—in more ways than one."

With a giggle, an honest-to-goodness giggle, she buried her face in his chest.

"It wasn't until Laurel called off the wedding and it didn't bother me in the least that I realized I was marrying her for the wrong reasons. Then I went over to your place, and it was as though I was seeing you for the first time. Clearly, through new eyes. It was startling and invigorating and humbling…and I knew, without a shadow of a doubt, that I wanted you. Not just for a night or a weekend or even a year, but forever."

Heart stuttering in her chest, Kara lifted her head and met his gaze. "Say that again," she told him.

The corners of his mouth lifted. "Which part?"

"All of it," she said on a sigh. "Or maybe just the highlights."

Running his fingers through her hair, then lingering to toy with the ends of the curls, he said, "Here are the important bullet points: I love you. I want you. I need you."

He punctuated each declaration with a soft but firm kiss to her lips. Kisses that melted her bones and turned her knees to jelly.

"Now answer one of my questions," he murmured. "Do *you* love *me?*"

Her lashes fluttered and the air skittered from her lungs. "More than anything," she told him.

"And you don't think I'm after your money or your family name? Especially considering that I've amassed a rather large financial portfolio in my own right, and my parents' roots—the only parents who matter, at any rate—go back at least as far as the Kincaids'."

His face hardened, his eyes going dark, but she knew he wasn't really angry. Annoyed that anyone could ever believe that, maybe, but not mad. Still, she couldn't resist teasing him.

"I don't know," she said with an exaggerated sigh. "We are *really* rich. And there are *a lot* of men out there who want me. I'm irresistible."

The corner of his mouth twitched, and she knew she had him.

"You are that," he agreed, obvious humor slipping into his tone. "But I'm afraid I have to have you—money, well-respected Southern name, and all. So what can I do to convince you? Give up my vast fortune? Shout it from the highest rooftop? Eat a bug?"

She just barely managed to hold back a chuckle. "You *could* eat a bug."

He scowled at her, letting her know that wasn't going to happen.

"All right, then, I have an idea," she said.

Standing on tiptoe, she looped her arms around his neck, getting as close as possible. To her delight, he did the same at the small of her back.

"I haven't gotten around to canceling everything for your and Laurel's nuptials." She'd taken care of some of the items on the list, but then got sidetracked by his work-weekend-turned-sexual-rendezvous and the emotional upheaval that went along with it.

"So…if you love me as much as you claim, and truly want to be with me for the rest of your life…" Her entire body hummed with that knowledge and the soul-deep contentment it brought. "You could keep your original wedding date, but marry me instead."

His eyes widened, then began to twinkle. "Marry you? Next month?"

"Two weeks from now, actually."

"Hmm. I don't know, that's awfully soon," he said with mock indecision.

"It is. But think of it this way—once you tie me to you legally, I'll be forced to take your name…and half of your money. It's the perfect solution to all of our problems."

He laughed. "You may be right about that. And something tells me you're going to enjoy spending my money."

"Mmm-hmm. Almost as much as I enjoy spending my own."

"I'll bet." Then he tipped his head, seeming to consider something. "You know, maybe I should go back to Laurel, after all. She may not be as hot as you are, but she might end up costing me less in the long run."

Eyes wide, Kara pulled back and punched him hard in the chest. "Hey! Be careful, bub, or I'll rescind my offer. Then you'll not only be without the hot Kincaid sister, but I'll stick you with all the cancellation fees for the rest of the wedding arrangements."

"We can't have that," he said, shaking his head slowly back and forth. "I guess I have no choice—I'll have to marry you. But only if you promise to remain as sweet, smart, funny, beautiful, wonderful and amazing as you are at this very moment."

She tipped her head, rolled her eyes skyward and gave her best drawn-out Southern belle sigh. "I suppose I could do that. But *you* have to promise to always be as kind, smart, wonderful, patient, sexy and amazing as *you* are at this moment."

With the cocky, self-assured grin she'd fallen in love with so many years ago, he said, "Oh, I think I can handle that, darlin'."

And then he leaned down to kiss her, stealing her breath and taking her heart, her soul, her very being right along with it. When he broke off minutes later, they were gasping for breath.

Eli touched his brow to hers. "I want to take you home and make love to you. Make you mine, once and for all. My place or yours, I don't care which."

She wanted that, too. So much, she was trembling.

"I'm already yours," she told him, and meant every word. "But what about the party? Your guests might notice if their host suddenly disappears."

He groaned, turning his head slightly to check on the birthday celebration. The children were still playing, eating, having fun…but several adult eyes were on them, curiosity running rampant.

"I think you're right," he said. "Our absence would definitely be noted. And commented upon."

Resting the tips of her fingers on one side of his strong, smooth face, she pressed a light kiss to the other. "Tell you what," she said. "Introduce me to the children so I can get a feel for their personalities and what kind of gifts they might like in the future. After a bit, we'll make our apologies, and you can take me home—your place or mine—and have your way with me for the rest of the night."

One dark brow shot halfway to his hairline. "Now that's a plan I can get behind," he told her. "I can see why you're so good at your job, Miss Kincaid."

She met his raised brow with one of her own. "That's Soon-to-be Mrs. Houghton to you, sir."

He flashed her a wide grin, lifting her left hand to his mouth and kissing the spot on her finger where his ring would soon reside. A diamond temporarily, followed by a solid gold band for the rest of their lives.

"Yes, ma'am," he said softly. "It certainly is."

Seventeen

Kara stood outside the front door of her mother's home—also known as the Kincaid Mansion—on Montagu Street, fidgeting like a mouse in a room full of traps ready to spring. The heat from Eli's strong, broad body was close at her back, adding to that of her growing anxiety and the warm April afternoon.

"If you don't calm down," he whispered just above her right ear, his hands resting lightly at her hips, "they're going to know something is up the minute you walk through the door."

"I know." But that didn't keep her nerves from jangling or her pulse from jumping in her throat. Her fingers tightened on the container of homemade apple fritters she was carrying, for fear she might drop them.

"And that's if they don't notice the ring right off."

The lump in her throat plummeted to her stomach. Oh, lord. She hadn't needed to hear that.

After the birthday party at the park, Eli had indeed taken her home—to his apartment, as it turned out—and made love to her *all...night...long....* Over and over, until she was weak in the knees...and the spine...and the brain stem...and everywhere in between.

The very next morning, he'd woken her with kisses that quickly led to another round of slow, languid sex, followed by breakfast in bed and the pronouncement that they were going ring shopping. As soon as he managed to stop touching her long enough to let her get dressed, they'd strolled hand in hand to the nearest jeweler's he'd approved of, where he'd only let her look at the trays of rings that they kept under lock and key. Nothing from the average, everyday display case for *his* bride-to-be, he'd declared.

She'd walked out with the biggest, most beautiful engagement ring she'd ever seen. A three-carat, princess-cut diamond in a one-of-a-kind yellow gold and platinum floral setting with even more smaller diamonds dotting the band, it was nearly blinding in its brilliance. Showier than she would normally wear, as well, but she absolutely loved it, Eli had insisted, and for once she wasn't going to worry about what anyone else might think. She was blissfully in love, happier than she'd ever been before in her life, and wanted to soak up every minute, every detail, every exquisite sensation.

Which was easier said than done, since she hadn't yet told her family about the latest developments in her personal life, and wasn't entirely sure how they would take it. On top of that, her mother had *just* been cleared on Thursday of all charges connected to her father's murder.

This was the first Sunday dinner they would be attending since the news had broken, and the Kincaid family was sure to be in a celebratory mood. That was good; she hoped they would be equally willing to celebrate when she announced that Eli had asked her to marry him—well, she'd asked him, but he'd readily agreed, thank goodness—she'd said yes, and they intended to follow through with most of Laurel's original wedding plans so that they could hold the ceremony next week.

Her mother was sure to think there was a reason for the rush down the aisle—especially since Lily was four months along with Daniel's child—but Kara simply wanted to be married. To Eli. She'd spent most of her life longing for him; she didn't want to waste a single minute more *not* being legally bound to him and beginning their life together as man and wife. She also had to admit that—because Laurel had seemed so disinterested throughout the planning stages—the wedding Kara arranged for her sister was very close to her own idea of a dream wedding.

She would be picking out her own gown, of course, and adjusting the color scheme and guest list somewhat. But otherwise, everything that was already in place was darn near perfect.

If only her father could have been there to give her away, it would be.

"Do you want me to go in first?" Eli asked, as though they were tromping off to the gallows and he was offering to get in line ahead of her. "Or would you rather we skip out altogether? We could call and tell them we're stuck in traffic...or out of town on business...or were mauled by bears."

She turned on him, eyes wide. "How in the world would we ever be mauled by bears?"

He shrugged. "I'm just trying to help, sugar. If you don't want to tell them about our engagement, I'll understand. We can even push back the wedding."

"No!" Spinning around, she faced him, separated only by the dessert container that she was clutching like a life preserver. "We're getting married next week if we have to fly to Vegas and elope. I'm just nervous about how they'll react, considering that—until earlier this month—you were engaged to Laurel. Some of the details are going to be a little hard for folks to swallow."

"And to explain."

Her mouth twisted with frustration. "You see my dilemma."

He smiled gently, lifting a hand to brush a stray curl away from her face and behind her ear. The gesture was becoming something of a habit for him...but a habit she liked. A lot.

"Our dilemma," he said. "We're a package deal now, darlin'. But I don't think we have anything to worry about. Your family loves me. And your sister is the one who dumped me, not the other way around, so I've got that whole 'innocent party,' 'sympathy card' thing going for me."

She chuckled. "You're right. They're going to feel sorry for you. If we can play on that, we may have a shot at catching them off guard with our news."

"Here's another idea," he suggested. "We could tell them we're engaged, tell them we're hijacking Laurel's wedding plans, tell them they're invited…and then tell them we love each other, whether they approve of the circumstances of our relationship or not."

Grasping her upper arms and tugging her slightly toward him, until the apple fritters nudged at them both, he added, "I've waited too long to find you, Kara. I'm not going to let anyone—not even your family—make me feel guilty or ashamed of how we got together."

He looked positively ferocious. Brows drawn together, mouth pulled taut. She suspected he could take on those imaginary bears, if they showed up now and tried to maul them, and come out of the skirmish without a scratch.

But instead of being intimidated by his dark scowl, it calmed her. Warmed her from her very center outward, and seemed to wash away every last one of her frazzled nerves.

Smiling from ear to ear, she reached up to trace the line of his jaw. "Have I told you lately how much I love you?"

His features softened and he winked. "I recall you saying something along those lines this morning while you were on top of me, riding me like—"

Slapping a hand over his mouth, she shushed him, struggling not to flush with embarrassment even as a sudden wave of erotic memory and equally erotic need crashed over her.

"Now cut that out or we'll never make it inside," she told him sternly, doing her best to ignore the wicked sparkle in his brown eyes. "And for the record, I *do* love you, and I don't feel the least bit guilty about or ashamed of how we got together, either. I only wish we'd been smart enough to do it a decade ago."

Plucking the fritter container out of her hands, he held it aside and dragged her against his chest. He kissed her on the lips, long and slow, licking off all of the color she'd just applied in the car, she was sure.

"Don't worry," he murmured into her mouth, "we'll spend the next decade making up for lost time, I promise."

Then he turned her around and gave her a little shove toward the front door. "Now let's go inside before you get cold feet again."

Following his instructions—not quite as reluctantly this time—she opened the door and entered the wide foyer. Eli had just closed the door behind them, when Laurel appeared in front of them, almost as though she'd been waiting just around the corner, ready to pounce the second they arrived.

With a sigh and rolling eyes, she threw up her hands. "There you are. I was about to send out a search party."

"We aren't that late," Kara insisted.

"No, but Matt and Susannah are in Georgia with Flynn. You *know* how Mama likes everyone to attend Sunday dinner when they can, so she's been frantic you weren't going to show."

"I told her I'd be here." She took the dessert container back from Eli and held it up for Laurel to see. "I even brought apple fritters."

Laurel's gaze darted from Kara to Eli and back again. Then a smug smile started to spread across her face.

"Hello, Eli. It's nice to see you."

"You, too, Laurel."

"So…I take it everything worked out okay between the two of you," she said without a hint of subtlety.

"Everything is fine," Kara told her, and left it at that.

Apple fritters in hand, she started toward the dining room. As she passed her sister, she mouthed, "I'll tell you later."

In the dining room, the long mahogany table was already

set with steaming plates and platters and bowls of amazing-looking food. Which was nothing surprising; Kara had grown up with meals like this, especially on Sunday afternoons. Chicken-fried steak, okra gumbo, red rice, potato salad, grits topped with real butter, pumpkin biscuits…and later, the ap-ple-pecan fritters Kara had made from scratch while trying to fend off advances from Eli—to both her body and her baking.

"Kara!" her mother cried from her seat at the head of the table. She pushed back her chair and came around to give her a hug. "I'm so glad you made it. And Eli…"

Elizabeth beamed up at him, not settling for a polite hand-shake, but wrapping her arms around him, as well.

"You're just in time. We were about to sit down and say grace, but I didn't want to start without you."

"We wouldn't miss it," Kara assured her.

Her brother RJ and Brooke, his fiancée of less than a month, as well as the youngest Kincaid sister, Lily, and her new hus-band, Daniel Addison, were already seated. But as Eli and the other women neared the table, both RJ and Daniel rose.

RJ greeted Kara with a kiss to the cheek, then moved to hold Elizabeth's chair for her while Daniel helped Laurel and Eli helped Kara. True Southern gentlemen down to the bone.

Once they were all settled and had said grace, food was passed around until everyone's plate was full. While they ate, they discussed a number of events that had impacted the Kin-caid family over the past few months. The charges against Elizabeth being dropped…Lily and Daniel learning they were expecting a girl……RJ and Brooke's recent engagement and talk of either an engagement party or shifting straight to wed-ding plans—they couldn't decide which.

The general consensus, of course, was that Kara would be the one to help each of them plan whatever type of event they decided to throw. From party to wedding to wedding recep-tion, and everything in between, she was the Kincaids' go-to gal for that sort of thing. And she was happy to help.

But as the conversation turned to upcoming nuptials, she

couldn't remain silent any longer. Eli might say he didn't mind putting off the announcement of their engagement or even their wedding, but *she* did, and the first step toward getting the deed done was sharing the news with her family.

She was lucky they hadn't already noticed the ring sitting on her left hand like a live canary. But then, she'd spent most of the meal hiding it on her lap beneath the table.

Swallowing a last bite of potato salad, she washed it down with a sip of sweet tea, then cleared her throat to get her family's attention.

"Actually," she told them, reaching for Eli's hand beneath, "Eli and I have a bit of news to share, as well."

The entire table grew silent, all eyes on her…with the occasional roll to Eli and then back.

"Eli has asked me to marry him, and I've accepted. Not only that," she rushed to get in before the collective gasp that filled the room could turn into a free-for-all of questions and comments and demands for details, "but we've decided to go ahead and follow through with Laurel's original wedding plans. So I hope none of you have made alternate plans for next weekend."

As soon as she finished, chaos erupted. The women squealed—especially when they saw her ring—and started talking at the speed of light. The men stood and came around to shake Eli's hand and slap him on the back.

In only a matter of minutes, Kara started to wonder why she'd ever been anxious about telling her family to begin with. They were wonderful and supportive and genuinely happy for her, just as they'd been all her life.

The fact that Eli had been engaged to marry Laurel less than a month ago, or that he was suddenly set to marry Kara when they'd known each other forever, but never so much as flirted before didn't even come up, though she was sure there would be questions—*lots* of questions—later. Her mother and brother and sisters simply accepted that she was an adult, and knew her own mind and heart well enough to know what—and who—she wanted.

While the men formed a small circle in one corner of the room for "manly talk," Elizabeth insisted they needed to celebrate, dragging Lily and Brooke with her to the kitchen. Kara didn't know if they would return with wine flutes and a bottle of champagne (and something equally festive, but non-alcoholic for Lily) or simply coffee and her apple-pecan fritters arranged on a fancy silver tray.

Rather than follow along, though, Kara grabbed Laurel's elbow and held her back. The one thing that continued to plague her mind was that her older sister might still be harboring feelings for Eli, despite her continued assertion to the contrary.

She believed her sister, and yet…how could anyone *not* be head over heels in love with Eli? How could any woman—even Laurel—be ready to marry him, only to turn around and be content to see him spend his life with someone else?

Kara would certainly never be able to sit back and watch while something like that happened. Not now that she'd been with him, given him her heart and soul.

"Are you sure you're all right with this?" she asked in a low voice so nobody else would hear.

Laurel gave a light, carefree chuckle. "Of course. Oh, Kara, I'm so happy for you!" She grabbed Kara up for another quick hug. "Eli and I were never meant to be together, but you…you two are positively glowing. You're like separate electrical currents coming together to light up an entire city block."

Kara's throat tightened and she blinked to hold back tears. "I love him so much, Laurel. I never wanted to steal him from you, but seeing him with you was killing me."

"I can imagine," Laurel said with an even heartier laugh. "But you didn't steal him from me. I gave him to you—freely and without hesitation. Or maybe Eli simply wised up and realized who it was he truly wanted."

"Thank you."

"I do have a question for you, though." Laurel tipped her

head. "Since you're recycling most of my wedding plans—which is a fabulous idea, don't even *think* about feeling guilty for that!—can I be your maid of honor? I mean, you were going to be mine, so it's only fair."

"Yes!" It was Kara's turn to squeal. "Oh, yes, I'd love that! And Mama can be there, too, now that the charges against her have been dropped, thank goodness."

"It's all going to be absolutely perfect," Laurel agreed. "In fact, you've inspired me. I'm tired of being so cautious and always playing it safe. You jumped into love with Eli feet-first, and look how things turned out. Meanwhile, I nearly married him because it was comfortable and easy. I need to be more spontaneous, take more risks. Live life instead of letting it just roll by day after day."

Nibbling at the inside of her lip, Kara said, "Taking a chance did pay off for me, but…just be careful, okay? I'm all for spontaneity, but don't go crazy or do anything dangerous."

"No danger," Laurel assured her. "I want to add a little spice to my life, not jump out of a plane head-first."

A moment later, the other women burst back into the room with champagne *and* coffee to go with Kara's fritters. Elizabeth also brought the phone with her so she could call Matthew and tell him the good news.

Soon after she'd spoken with her brother, Kara felt strong arms come around her waist from behind, and she was tugged back against the solid wall of Eli's chest. She smiled, leaning into him with a sigh.

"Since I know my chances of ever being right again once we're married are slim to none," he teased, "I'd like it noted that I *was* right about this. You had nothing to be nervous about with your family."

"You were right," she admitted. "I'll endeavor to listen to you and trust in your impeccable wisdom from now on."

He chuckled just above her ear. "We'll see how long that lasts. I'm guessing not much past the honeymoon."

She gave a little *hmph* beneath her breath, only to feel him press a kiss to her temple.

"Speaking of honeymoons," he murmured, "have you given any thought to where you'd like to go for ours?"

"Oh, lord," she moaned, leaning against him even more. "Everything's been happening so fast, I forgot all about that. Maybe we could go back to Seabrook Island and hide out in your suite again."

Turning her in his arms, he tipped her head up and stared down into her eyes while tracing the outline of her bottom lip with his thumb.

"Ocean Breezes may be one of *the* premiere oceanside resorts in the continental United States," he said proudly, "but it doesn't hold the greatest of track records for us, and I don't want to take any chances. Not with our honeymoon."

He made a good point, although she had a lot of wonderful, spine-tingling, swoon-inducing memories of her time there with him, too.

He must have been thinking the same thing, because a wicked glint filled his eyes. "Give some thought to something truly decadent. The French Riviera. The Greek Isles. The coast of Spain."

Her heart leapt higher at each of his suggestions. She could picture them touring any one—or all—of those, and the images were hugely romantic.

"Yes, yes and yes," she told him, puckering her lips to kiss the pad of his thumb as it neared the center of her mouth. "I'm not sure we should travel so far away right now, though. Not with Mama newly freed from suspicion and Daddy's murderer still on the loose."

Taking her hands, he threaded his fingers with hers, holding them down at their sides. "Then we'll put it off until we can do it right. But keep those locations in mind. I'll take you anywhere you like, for as long as you like. Provided we schedule plenty of time for me to get you alone. And naked. Several times a day."

"Thank you," she said, rising up to kiss him, wondering how she'd ever gotten so lucky as to end up with a man like this. Then again, she'd always known Eli Houghton was special. It was part of the reason she'd lusted after him for so long.

Pulling away, she fluttered her lashes and gave him her best come-hither look. "I'm not the least bit interested in fritters anymore, but if you split one with me and we gulp down a glass of champagne each, it will make Mama happy. Then I can come up with an excuse to get out of here, so you can take me home and get me naked. How does that sound, Mr. Houghton?"

His gaze smoldered, his brown eyes hot enough to singe the clothes from her body right in the middle of her mother's formal dining room.

"Better than a honeymoon, Soon-to-be Mrs. Houghton," he replied. The use of those names—Mr. and Soon-to-be Mrs.—had become a bit of an inside joke with them. The wedding was only a week away, and yet they couldn't seem to wait to be tied to each other in every way possible.

Lifting his arm, he studied the face of his expensive watch. "One hour. I'm counting down. If you haven't said goodbye to your family by then, I'm tossing you over my shoulder and carrying you off caveman-style."

A shiver stole through her at the thought of that. It might be worth shocking her mother and brother and sisters—not to mention their significant others—just to see if he really would do as he threatened…and then reap the benefits of those Neanderthal-ish tendencies of his.

Leaning up on tiptoe, she put her mouth to his ear and whispered, "If you keep looking at me like that, I might just let you."

Her reward was a deep growl and his hands coming up to squeeze her bottom possessively. She chuckled, pressing a quick kiss to his rugged cheek and breaking away to get in as much family time as he would allow before following through on his warning.

Oh, Eli was definitely the man for her. It might have taken

her half her life to admit it and then work up the courage to claim him as her own, but now that she had him…

She was never, ever letting go.

* * * * *

*Turn the page for an exclusive short story
by USA TODAY bestselling author Day Leclaire.
Then look for the next installment of*
DYNASTIES: THE KINCAIDS
*ONE DANCE WITH THE SHEIKH,
by Tessa Radley.
Wherever Harlequin Books are sold.*

THE KINCAIDS: JACK AND NIKKI
PART IV

"You've been so quiet."

Jack Sinclair joined Nikki Thomas on the deck off his beach house bedroom. Coming up behind her, he encircled her with his arms. The long, lovely sweep of her back fit perfectly against his chest and the sweet curve of her backside shifted against him, arousing him in a way no other woman had. Ever. Why her, and no one else?

"I guess I have a lot on my mind," she admitted.

"Work?"

A tiny sigh escaped her, sounding almost painful in its intensity. "Always."

Together they watched the rising moon sit on the line of rolling breakers, huge and squat, as though attempting to keep the restless sea under control. Of course, that was no more possible than controlling the desperation that exploded between them whenever they came together. The violent need and endless yearning had governed their two-month-long affair. And while Jack suspected they'd both anticipated it would fade over time, it only grew stronger with each passing week.

Nikki was his. Had been his since she first appeared beneath the balcony of the Read and Write literacy auction where she'd bid a thousand dollars for a single dinner date with him—as well as a wish of her choice. Of course, that one date had led to two months of dates, her wish not yet made or fulfilled. She'd continued to be his over that time, their headlong tumble one neither had anticipated.

The moon crept higher into the night sky, silvering a slice of the dark ocean and playing across the foam capping the surging waves. Nikki turned to Jack, wrapped him up in bewitching feminine warmth, then gently, tenderly fit her mouth to his. He felt the heat of passion beneath the softness, knew it would take no more than a simple nudge to move it up a notch. But for some reason, he simply wanted to enjoy the slow, easy slide that spoke of more than sex. That acknowledged the build of a relationship that fired on levels he never thought possible.

He filled his lungs with her sigh of pleasure and teased inward between her parted lips. Sank into her. Relished the sweetness and generosity. Her openness. She initiated a lazy dance, one he followed just as lazily. They drifted across the deck toward the French doors leading to his bedroom. The moon followed them, lighting a silvery pathway. It frosted her skin, giving it a pearlescent gleam and slipped through her thin silk nightgown to outline glorious womanly curves that tempted him beyond reason.

"I'm sorry if I've been a little out of it." She slanted him an amused look, her sapphire-blue eyes glinting in the moonlight. "If it makes you feel any better I'm all here now."

"Well… I was going to suggest you lay back and think of England, but I'm not quite sure what that has to do with my future plans for you."

She chuckled. "I believe that was a suggestion given to British women during the Victorian Era when it came to fulfilling their marital obligations." Her arms tightened around his neck and she caught his lower lip between his teeth, giving it a light tug. "The only thing I plan to think about is you and just what I'm going to do to you."

His voice deepened. Roughened. "And what's that?"

Nikki lifted on tiptoe and put her mouth close to Jack's ear, the warmth of her breath threatening the last of his control. Then her whispered suggestions totally shredded it. A growl rumbled through his chest and he snatched her into his arms and dumped her onto the bed. He ripped her nightgown from her body, made short work of his own sweats and was over and in her welcoming body with a speed that left them both gasping. His name clung to her damp, swollen lips, her want for him burning in her gaze, her unstinting response to his possession driving him to new heights.

He couldn't get enough of this woman. Didn't think he'd ever get enough. As though she could read his thoughts, she moaned in pleasure. "More. No matter how much or how often, I'm always ready for more." She cupped his face, took everything he offered and gave all she had in return. "Only with you. Always with you."

And somehow Jack suspected it would be that way for the rest of their lives.

"Nikki, are you paying attention?"

She jumped, her gaze flashing to RJ Kincaid's, guilt sweeping through her. Oh, damn. What had he asked? She did a quick rewind, relieved to discover that her brain had been recording the conversation, despite her distraction. Police update. He wanted a police update on the investigation into his father's murder.

"I've spoken to Detective McDonough about the camera surveillance discovered showing Jack Sinclair's vintage Aston Martin parked at a lot near The Kincaid Group at the time of your father's death."

"Why isn't Sinclair in custody?" RJ demanded, the fierce expression in his eyes identical to Jack's—as well as to their father's. They were half brothers, "the Legitimates," as Jack referred to them, Reginald Kincaid's legal offspring, while Jack was the product of a decades-long affair with Angela Sinclair, Reginald's mistress. "The police were quick enough to arrest my mother on far less evidence."

Nikki couldn't help it. She flinched at the idea of Jack being dragged off to jail in handcuffs. He wasn't guilty. There wasn't a single doubt in her mind. You couldn't share such an intimate relationship with a man and not know who he was at his core. And while he might be one of the most ruthless men she'd ever met, clearly bent on revenge against his half siblings, that revenge would take a legal form. Like taking over the family business thanks to the forty-five percent interest he'd inherited in TKG upon his father's death. Of course, if he managed to win control of the business, his first act would be to fire RJ, Matthew and Laurel Kincaid.

Nikki sighed. "I've been in touch with Charles—Detective McDonough." He and her late father had been partners for years, before her father had gone down in the line of duty. "Jack claims he was at work at the time of your father's murder and has a number of employees who back him up."

RJ paced the length of the conference room, moving with all the grace and frustration of a caged panther, strengthening his resemblance to his half brother. How many times had she seen Jack pace like that while snapping instructions into his cell phone in regard to his own business, Carolina Shipping, a direct competitor to The Kincaid Group?

"Sinclair's guilty. We all know it. It has to be him. He must have found out about the forty-five percent share of TKG he stood to inherit. God knows, he's been after revenge for years because my father refused to publicly recognize Sinclair as his son. And when he wasn't good enough to beat us by pitting his business against ours, head-to-head, he killed Dad in order to take revenge the only way left to him."

More than anything, Nikki longed to argue with him. But she didn't dare. She was The Kincaid Group's corporate investigator and it was her job to research Jack on their behalf. She'd been given the assignment after the two of them had met at the literacy bachelor auction for Read and Write, and for the past two months she'd walked a tightrope between her feelings for Jack versus her obligations to her employer.

Even worse, Reginald Kincaid had hired her after she'd been unjustly fired by her previous employer. Reginald had believed in her when no one else had. She owed him then and still felt an unshakable loyalty and obligation to the family and business he left behind.

She took her time responding to RJ, allowing her gaze to drift over the three Kincaid siblings currently gathered in the conference room. "While I understand your feelings, the police need evidence. You want your father's killer found. That's only natural. But if you insist they focus their attention in any one direction you run the risk of having them miss something that would lead them to the person responsible. Is it Jack?" She lifted her shoulder in as casual a shrug as she could pull off. "It's possible, though current evidence is to the contrary."

"It's Jack," RJ snapped.

Matt gave a slow nod. She caught a hint of sympathy in his gaze and knew why. He was aware she'd gone out with Jack, as was Laurel. In fact, Laurel knew just how deeply their involvement went. Only RJ remained oblivious. Oh, he was aware they'd dated because of the Read and Write auction. Matt had even asked her to use the time she spent with him to form an opinion of the man and obtain any and all possible information. But she doubted any of them realized just how far the relationship had progressed.

And once they knew?

She released her breath in a silent sigh. She'd be out of a job again. Worse, the instant Jack found out she was a Kincaid employee, what had become an incandescent affair would fizzle like a wet firecracker. And where would she end up? Without Jack and without a job. Probably served her right for not coming clean with both parties.

But how could she? More than anything she hoped to prove

to the Kincaids that Jack didn't deserve their enmity. Just as she hoped to coax Jack into giving his half brothers and sisters a chance. To see if he couldn't form—if not a familial relationship with them—then at least a cordial relationship, one that would prompt him to drop his plan of revenge...which at the current moment was to utterly destroy the Kincaids.

She gave RJ a calm, direct look. "You know I am totally committed to finding out who murdered your father. Totally committed," she repeated. "And I will continue to do everything Detective McDonough will allow in order to help the police with their investigation, as well as research every possible avenue available to me independently."

Some of the tension eased from RJ's body. "Well, I can't ask for more than that, can I?"

Laurel cleared her throat. She was a gorgeous woman who had inherited her striking bone structure, vivid green eyes and deep, auburn hair from her mother, Elizabeth. She spared Nikki a brief, sympathetic glance before addressing her brothers. "We're all frustrated. We expected this to be resolved long ago. We have a board meeting coming up in less than two months that will decide the fate of The Kincaid Group, which has us all on edge." This time she addressed Nikki. "I appreciate everything you've done. When you're personally involved in the situation, it's very difficult to maintain an emotional distance."

Nikki winced. Okay, she could read between those lines. "Is there anything else?" she asked quietly.

RJ released a long sigh. "No, there's nothing else." He offered a swift, charming smile. "Sorry if I came down too hard on you. You're doing a great job."

But she wasn't. How could she when she remained so conflicted? She'd just do the best she could for everyone involved and hope that Charles McDonough found the real murderer. Laurel paused long enough to give her a brief hug.

"Hang in there. This will all work out," she whispered before exiting. "Sometimes you just have to decide to follow your heart instead of doing what everyone expects of you."

Nikki closed her eyes, tears pressing hard. If only she could believe that. How she longed to believe that. But somehow she suspected the situation would get far worse before it ever got better.

If it ever got better.

"I've already told you, Detective," Jack stated evenly. "I was here at the time my father was murdered."

Charles McDonough nodded. He was a strong, well-dressed black man with a gleaming shaved head, and calm, serious dark eyes that reflected his intelligence and determination. "Unfortunately for you, Mr. Sinclair, no one was actually in the room with you."

Jack fought back a flash of impatience. "Granted, my employees weren't in my office every minute of that time, but I couldn't have left the building without being seen or been gone as long as it must have taken without someone noticing my absence."

Charles gave another slow nod and made a notation in his neat, tidy handwriting. "You do have a private exit," he observed.

Jack fought back a flash of temper, well aware it wouldn't help his case. "True. But I never used it that night, certainly not to murder my own father."

"And yet your Aston Martin was in a lot near The Kincaid Group headquarters at the time of the murder." The detective's gaze locked with Jack's, piercing straight through him, warning of a dogged and unrelenting nature. "Did you loan your car to someone?"

"No."

"Have you ever loaned that car to someone else?"

"Never."

Charles smiled, for the first time revealing the man beneath the cop. "Don't blame you," he said. "Don't think I'd let anyone so much as breathe on it."

Jack relaxed enough to return the smile. "Men can be foolish about their toys."

"Yes." And suddenly the cop was back. "So explain how one of your toys—a toy you don't allow anyone else to touch—turned up where it shouldn't have been? If you didn't drive it elsewhere that night, then someone else had possession of your keys or ignition fob. That someone was able to enter your company parking lot and remove your car with no one stopping or questioning him. And then he returned both the car and the keys, with you none the wiser. I find that…odd. Don't you?"

"The lot isn't gated."

"And the keys?"

Jack shook his head. "Detective, I can't explain it, as I'm sure you're aware. I can only repeat that I was here, working on a special project. I've given you the name of the employees who were with me at that time helping with the Berner project. Most were in and out of this office at various times during the evening. It was common knowledge that I planned to work late that night. In fact, I was working late most nights due to a large, complicated project. My car was in its usual place when I finished for the night and left the building. I can't explain how it was spotted in a parking lot near The Kincaid Group at that particular time unless it was someone else's Aston Martin. I assume you've considered that possibility and already ruled it out."

McDonough didn't confirm or deny the assumption. He simply nodded, flipped his notebook closed and stood. "Please remain available, Mr. Sinclair. I'm sure I'll have more questions in the near future."

The Southern version of "don't leave town." "Of course," Jack agreed and stood as well. The two men shook hands before the detective departed.

The second McDonough departed, Jack's assistant entered

the office and dropped a file on his desk. "Hang in there, boss. This will all work out," she said with a sympathetic look.

He spared her a brief smile. "Thanks, Gail."

He wanted to believe that. Really wanted to believe it. But somehow he suspected the situation would get far worse before it ever got better.

If it ever got better.

Nikki exited The Kincaid Group office building, just as Elizabeth Kincaid and two of her daughters, Lily and Kara, approached. All were chatting and laughing. As the women drew level, Elizabeth paused and introduced her daughters, though Nikki had already met Lily at the bachelor auction back in January. Elizabeth appeared relaxed and energized, a far cry from the anguished, drawn woman of the past four months. No doubt it was due to her being released from police custody for the murder of her late husband, Reginald.

"Kara is an events planner," Elizabeth explained. "She owns Prestige Events."

Nikki smiled warmly. "I've heard wonderful things about your company."

"And she's engaged," Lily added. Her blue eyes gleamed with mischief. "To Eli Houghton. They marry this next weekend."

"But, I thought—" Nikki blinked. Last she'd heard Eli's engagement to Laurel had ended less than a month before. Since then he and Kara had apparently fallen in love—because it was crystal clear that the bubbly middle daughter was ecstatically happy. Since everyone else appeared equally happy, Nikki could only assume it had been an amicable transfer of bridegrooms. "Best wishes, Kara," she said and meant it.

"Thanks. We're about to go drag Laurel away from her desk and finalize wedding plans over food and drinks. She's offered to be my maid of honor."

With a cheerful wave, the women continued on their way. She felt genuinely happy for the Kincaids. They'd been through a terrible ordeal. But now that Elizabeth had been released on bail, Nikki worried that Jack would become the center of the investigative whirlwind. There simply weren't that many people who benefitted from Reginald's demise. Clearly, Jack was the forerunner in that regard and she knew, both from what Charles McDonough had said—as well as what he hadn't said—that the police were looking long and hard at Reginald's eldest son.

More than anything she wanted to find Jack. As though in response to her silent wish her cell phone rang with the ring tone she used exclusively for him. "Where are you?" he asked abruptly.

"Not far from home. Problem?"

"I could use you, a drink and food, in that order."

She smiled. "I think I can help you with that. Do you want to eat in or out?"

"In. Definitely in."

By the time she arrived home a fine mist clung to the city and the wind carried a chilly edge. They didn't often spend the evening at her place, despite its convenient location, perhaps because the row house didn't offer as much room as Jack's beach house. Or maybe it was because the furnishings were antique and somewhat delicate for a man. Or possibly it was a territorial problem, Jack unable to make his mark in the distinctly feminine environment. Tonight he made one of his rare exceptions.

They entered the small foyer and to her amusement both of their gazes flashed to a section of the wall where they'd collided during their second kiss—a chaste embrace that had exploded into an unexpected wildfire of desire. It had been that way when they first kissed on the night of the charity auction, flamed higher during that crazy second kiss and had continued to build ever since.

"Would you prefer to order out?" Nikki asked. "Or would you like me to throw something together? I probably have enough in the fridge for omelets." Maybe.

"Right now I just want you."

All he had to do was touch her to send her up in flames. His kiss tasted of desperation and need, his hands relentless in expressing that need and driving her own to the breaking point. Their clothing created a trail of passion leading upstairs to her bedroom. While the bed cupped them in silk and softness, the deepening night encased them in a protective dusk. Want perfuming the air, their husky cries lending music to their passionate dance. And when the moment was spent and the fires banked, they clung, two hearts beating in synchronicity, male and female locked together in perfect accord.

"You make it so much easier," he whispered. "I don't know how or why. But I don't think I could get through this without you."

"Get through what, Jack? What's happened?"

He rolled onto his back and rested his head on his folded arms. A pale wedge of light from the hallway sliced across the upper portion of his face, silvering his robin's-egg-blue eyes. Hardness glittered there, as it so often did. But she knew him well enough to see the pain that lurked beneath. The intense grief. The Kincaids weren't the only ones to lose their father. Jack had lost his, too.

"McDonough came to see me today."

"And?"

She caught a glimpse of a smile, though it contained little humor. "I've been told not to leave town."

"Oh, Jack," she whispered, reaching for him, telling him with a single touch that she was there for him. "Why? What do they have on you?"

He rolled onto his side to face her, feathering his hand through the silken length of her dark hair, then tracing the curve of her cheek. In the two months they'd been together she'd noticed that he had a need to touch, to stroke, to maintain a physical connection between them even during sleep. It was one of the qualities she loved about him. "Someone helped themselves to my car the night of Dad's murder and parked it near The Kincaid Group office building."

She stilled and tiptoed into what promised to become a minefield, praying he didn't pick up on her tension. "Who could have taken it?"

"That's the million dollar question, one I'd love to have answered." He'd finished tracing the angles of her face and crept lower, following the line of her neck to the sensitive joining of her shoulder. He smiled at the helpless shiver that rippled through her. "So would the police."

"They think it's you." She didn't bother to phrase it as a question.

His hand stilled briefly. "I suspect McDonough does, yes."

"How do they know your car was parked near The Kincaid Group?"

"They have a photo from a security camera I guess. Maybe video." A frown etched across his brow and his hand shifted, continued to stroke. "What I don't get is… If they have a photo or video, why don't they also have evidence of who was driving the car? That's all it would take to clear me."

"Good question." A very good question. One she'd be certain to ask Charles. "Who do you think killed your father?"

He closed his eyes, his expression turning grim. "I wish I knew. I can't imagine who'd do such a thing." He looked at her then, allowing his grief to leak through. "I could almost understand it when the police thought his wife had shot him. If she'd found out about my mother and they'd argued…"

"This wasn't a crime of passion," Nikki objected. "At least, it wasn't executed in a passionate manner."

"No, I came to that realization as well, which is why I have trouble suspecting any of the Kincaids. Someone had it in for Dad. As much as I despise the Legitimates, I can't see any of them pulling the trigger." He grimaced. "Not even RJ, though I don't suppose he feels the same way about me."

She almost answered, catching back the words in the nick of time. "Have you talked to him about it?"

"Of course not. All of our dealings have been strictly business-related. I requested and received a report on The Kincaid Group's assets, expenses, projected growth, as well as a comprehensive customer list back in January. Since then all we've done is have a number of terse, bitter conversations about how to handle the running of the business. It's clear we both hope to take control at the June board meeting." He traced his finger between the swell of her breasts and the edge of the sheet, then dipped beneath, causing her to inhale sharply. "I guess it all comes down to that missing ten percent."

The breath stuttered in her lungs. "What missing ten percent?" she asked.

"The Kincaids between them own forty-five percent of TKG stock. I now own the other forty-five percent. That leaves ten percent missing." He rolled on top of her, bracing himself so his forearms took most of his weight. "Though, not for long."

"No?"

His expression turned teasing and everything within her melted. "Nope. I'm going to hire someone to find the owner of those missing shares."

He lowered himself to her, inch by delicious inch, driving her insane with need. She opened to welcome him. "You are?" she asked weakly.

"Yes, I am. Someone I happen to know is a brilliant investigator and is well motivated to find the information I need."

She stiffened. Oh, no. Oh, please, no. "Who? Who is that?"

He joined their bodies, driving every coherent thought from her head…right up until he said, "Why, you, of course."

* * * * *

PASSION

Harlequin® *Desire*

COMING NEXT MONTH
AVAILABLE MAY 8, 2012

#2155 UNDONE BY HER TENDER TOUCH
Pregnancy & Passion
Maya Banks
When one night with magnate Cam Hollingsworth results in pregnancy, no-strings-attached turns into a tangled web for caterer Pippa Laingley.

#2156 ONE DANCE WITH THE SHEIKH
Dynasties: The Kincaids
Tessa Radley

#2157 THE TIES THAT BIND
Billionaires and Babies
Emilie Rose

#2158 AN INTIMATE BARGAIN
Colorado Cattle Barons
Barbara Dunlop

#2159 RELENTLESS PURSUIT
Lone Star Legacy
Sara Orwig

#2160 READY FOR HER CLOSE-UP
Matchmakers, Inc.
Katherine Garbera

REQUEST YOUR FREE BOOKS!
2 FREE NOVELS PLUS 2 FREE GIFTS!

Harlequin

Desire

ALWAYS POWERFUL, PASSIONATE AND PROVOCATIVE

YES! Please send me 2 FREE Harlequin Desire® novels and my 2 FREE gifts (gifts are worth about $10). After receiving them, if I don't wish to receive any more books, I can return the shipping statement marked "cancel." If I don't cancel, I will receive 6 brand-new novels every month and be billed just $4.30 per book in the U.S. or $4.99 per book in Canada. That's a saving of at least 14% off the cover price! It's quite a bargain! Shipping and handling is just 50¢ per book in the U.S. and 75¢ per book in Canada.* I understand that accepting the 2 free books and gifts places me under no obligation to buy anything. I can always return a shipment and cancel at any time. Even if I never buy another book, the two free books and gifts are mine to keep forever.

225/326 HDN FEF3

Name _____ (PLEASE PRINT)

Address _____ Apt. #

City _____ State/Prov. _____ Zip/Postal Code

Signature (if under 18, a parent or guardian must sign)

Mail to the **Reader Service:**
IN U.S.A.: P.O. Box 1867, Buffalo, NY 14240-1867
IN CANADA: P.O. Box 609, Fort Erie, Ontario L2A 5X3

Not valid for current subscribers to Harlequin Desire books.

Want to try two free books from another line?
Call 1-800-873-8635 or visit www.ReaderService.com.

* Terms and prices subject to change without notice. Prices do not include applicable taxes. Sales tax applicable in N.Y. Canadian residents will be charged applicable taxes. Offer not valid in Quebec. This offer is limited to one order per household. All orders subject to credit approval. Credit or debit balances in a customer's account(s) may be offset by any other outstanding balance owed by or to the customer. Please allow 4 to 6 weeks for delivery. Offer available while quantities last.

Your Privacy—The Reader Service is committed to protecting your privacy. Our Privacy Policy is available online at www.ReaderService.com or upon request from the Reader Service.

We make a portion of our mailing list available to reputable third parties that offer products we believe may interest you. If you prefer that we not exchange your name with third parties, or if you wish to clarify or modify your communication preferences, please visit us at www.ReaderService.com/consumerschoice or write to us at Reader Service Preference Service, P.O. Box 9062, Buffalo, NY 14269. Include your complete name and address.

to make her dizzy.

Cameron Hollingsworth was gorgeous, unpolished in a rough and totally sexy way, arrogant and so wrong for her. But there was something about the man that just did it for her.

She sighed. He was a luscious specimen of a male and he couldn't be any less interested in her.

Even so, she was itching to shake his world up a little.

Realizing she was spending far too much time mooning over Cameron, she grabbed another tray, took a deep breath to compose herself and then headed toward the living room.

And Cameron Hollingsworth.

Will Pippa shake up Cameron's world?
Find out in Maya Banks's passionate new novel

UNDONE BY HER TENDER TOUCH

Available May 2012 from Harlequin® Desire!

New York Times *and* USA TODAY *bestselling author*
Maya Banks presents book four in her miniseries
PREGNANCY & PASSION

UNDONE BY HER TENDER TOUCH

Available May 2012 from Harlequin® Desire!

"**W**ould you like some help?"

Pippa whirled around, still holding the bottle of champagne, and darn near tossed the contents onto the floor.

"Help?"

Cam nodded slowly. "Assistance? You look as though you could use it. How on earth did you think you'd manage to cater this event on your own?"

Pippa was horrified by his offer and then, as she processed the rest of his statement, she was irritated as hell.

"I'd hate for you to sully those pretty hands," she snapped. "And for your information, I've got this under control. The help didn't show. Not my fault. The food is impeccable, if I do say so myself. I just need to deliver it to the guests."

"I believe I just offered my assistance and you insulted me," Cam said dryly.

Her eyebrows drew together. Oh, why did the man have to be so damn delicious-looking? And why could she never perform the simplest functions around him?

"You're Ashley's guest," Pippa said firmly. "Not to mention you're used to being served, not serving others."

"How do you know what I'm used to?" he asked mildly.

She had absolutely nothing to say to that and watched in bewilderment as he hefted the tray up and walked out of the kitchen.

She sagged against the sink, her pulse racing hard enough